THE TROLL-DEMON WAR

THE TROLL WARS TRILOGY: BOOK ONE

LEAH R CUTTER

KNOTTED ROAD PRESS

The Troll-Demon War
The Troll Wars Trilogy: Book One
Copyright © 2019 Leah Cutter
All rights reserved
Published by Knotted Road Press
www.KnottedRoadPress.com

ISBN: 978-1-64470-039-6

Cover Art:
ID 24623341 © Prometeus | Depositphoto.com

Cover and interior design copyright © 2019 Knotted Road Press
http://www.KnottedRoadPress.com

Come someplace new…
If you'd like to be notified of new releases, sign up for my newsletter.

I will never spam you or use your email for nefarious purposes. You can also unsubscribe at any time.

http://www.LeahCutter.com/newsletter/

ALSO BY LEAH R CUTTER

Seattle Trolls

The Changeling Troll

The Princess Troll

The Fairy-Bridge Troll

The Troll-Demon War

The Troll-Human War

The Troll-Troll War

The Cassie Stories

Poisoned Pearls

Tainted Waters

Spoiled Harvest

Bloodied Ice

Tanish Empire Trilogy

The Glass Magician

The Desert Heart

The Ghost Dog

The Shadow Wars Trilogy

The Raven and the Dancing Tiger

The Guardian Hound

War Among the Crocodiles

CHAPTER ONE

Lars Sorgenfreys shivered in the cold depths of the hellish prison that the court had sentenced him to. The cell was purposefully too small—he couldn't expand his black, bat-like wings fully, the bare bones at the tops of the struts scraping painfully against the rocky ceiling. He was forced to constantly squat on his powerful legs. He could never straighten up and take a full stride. The yellowish scales that covered his chest itched and some had even flaked off, exposing the sensitive, pale-white flesh underneath. He had to be careful now not to burn himself with the black ichor that dripped from his long, forked tongue or to scratch himself with his long claws.

Sometimes, when standing grew to be too much and it felt as though weights had suddenly been attached to his chest and back, he collapsed onto the cold ground. That was just as bad. Though the floor looked like plain dirt, it felt like ice, sinking into his bones with pointed spikes.

At least the air had a nice sulfur smell to it. It was just the monotony of the scent that bothered Lars. He hadn't thought he'd miss clear skies and clean air as much as he did. Not eating also irked him. The spells that held him, and would keep him imprisoned for a century, also sustained him. He'd just grown used to the human schedule of three meals a day.

The worst part of his imprisonment, however, was the laughter.

Lars didn't know where his jailors got the laugh track from. Or maybe they continually sampled human audiences at comedy shows and piped in fresh mirth on a regular basis.

All that gaiety, *human* gaiety, made Lars grind his teeth and slash out at the impervious rock walls holding him.

It was the worst form of torture his jailors could have come up for a demon like Lars, one who was determined to see all of humanity grovel before him and finally be shoved back into their proper place on the food chain, with the demons on top, of course.

During his darkest nights, Lars felt as though the laughter was directed at *him*, as though all those humans were laughing at him and no one else.

Lars shivered again. He just could never get warm here. Kind of the point for a demon from hell. It was prison. He wasn't supposed to be *comfortable*. He'd failed to bring about the start of the Great War, and the one thing that demons hated more than anything else was failure.

This time though, he would succeed.

It had taken four years, but Lars' family had finally been able to bribe the right guards to get him a temporary reprieve. Once every ten days or so the magic holding Lars in his demon form was removed and he was able to take human form for a short while.

The original deal had been for Lars to stay that way for merely an hour; however, the guards occasionally forgot to recast the restriction spells right away. They'd let him stay in his human form for half a day the longest time.

Lars had gotten a lot accomplished then.

The cell he was imprisoned in was specifically designed to prevent him from using his demonic magic.

What the fools hadn't realized was that Lars had spent enough time on the human plane, in human form, to be able to pick up some *human* magical tricks.

Like the one for creating hidden pockets of space. While all magical creatures had some ability to access alternate planes, it had been the humans who'd developed it into an art form with their bags of holding and envelopes of space. Hell, Lars had even met human women who didn't have any magical abilities whatsoever yet had been able to carry more in their purses than should have been physically possible.

Those same purses made good bludgeons as well, something else Lars had discovered early on, much to his chagrin.

His focus today though, wasn't on his few failures. He was a big enough demon to admit he'd made some mistakes. Like not killing that damned princess troll Christine when he'd had the chance.

She'd tricked him, something he could almost admire in an enemy. Particularly from a troll, one of the races of the *kith and kin* who weren't particularly known for their intelligence.

Then again, Christine had been a changeling, raised as a human. Who were almost as tricky as demons. Lars could acknowledge that.

However, Lars had come up with a plan to use that trickiness against Christine, to force her to make mistakes.

And this time, he'd not only bring about the Great War, but ensure that the demons won.

Four races battled constantly for top rank on the planes of existence: the Host—the angels, the white elves, and the other disgusting do-gooders; the *kith and kin*—made up of the non-human races like orcs, trolls, were-creatures and shape shifters who should have always sided with their betters like Lars; humans—those stupid soft creatures who really shouldn't be allowed to rule anything; and demons—the greatest race of all.

Humans had won the last Great War over two thousand years before. The demons still proclaimed that they'd cheated, as the Host had brought in some outside help, claiming he was human but at the same time the son of God.

This time however, the demons would win. And they'd get their old allies, the *kith and kin*, to help.

Whether they realized it or not.

It had taken Lars another year of preparation—five years total in this hellish cell—to finally be ready to set the wheels into motion.

Wheels within wheels, plans within plans.

LARS NEVER KNEW WHEN THE SPELL FORCING HIM TO

stay in demon form would be relaxed. It was roughly once every ten days, but his jailors weren't precise about, well, anything.

How could they be? They were demons. Demons didn't specialize in precise, not like humans and angels.

The onslaught of laughter seemed particularly raucous that day. Lars shivered in his cell. How dare they? His jailors didn't understand how humiliating that laughter was. How torturous it seemed, as though each and every note of joy flayed more scales from Lars' back.

He had to get out of there. Soon. He'd always prided himself on holding his emotions in check, on being able to reply to any threat with a clever quip, never with fear or anger.

Not today. Today he wanted to tear the throat out of each and every human being he'd ever met or ever would meet.

The coldness of the dirt floor pressed in against the talons of his clawed feet, making them feel brittle, as though they'd shatter on the body of the first enemy he struck. His wings ached, as though they'd been infected with age and arthritis. Even his stomach roiled, disgusted by the constant rotten egg stench.

Lars howled in agony, fearing that it wouldn't stop, would never stop, that he'd be tortured here for all eternity. His ears hurt from the ringing sound, and his front claws tore uselessly at the rock walls of his cell.

When Lars found himself shrinking down, he continued his howls. They weren't going to kill him, were they? Crush his body like they'd been crushing his spirit?

It took him a few moments before he realized that he was transforming into his human form.

The change was painful, as it always was down here. On the human plane, the transformation was merely uncomfortable.

Here though, his wings felt as though they were being broken into smaller pieces and shoved down into his back. Scales flaked off his chest as it compacted, each leaving behind a burning spot that he could never cool. His jaw ached as his great fangs retracted. The sour taste of poison made him want to gag. Pain shot through his knees, feeling like nails were being hammered through them as his joints reversed, changing from that of a bird or a horse to that of a human.

Finally, the process was finished. Lars stood in the center of his cell, panting and naked. Sweat covered his pale torso. His blond hair fell over his eyes, which he assumed were still an icy blue. He'd always been called a handsome boy and had been able to flirt his way out of most trouble.

Now, his jaw felt stronger, more manly. His chest also seemed broader. Muscles lined his arms and his thighs looked powerful. All of the races obeyed the conservation of mass—a bigger creature usually looked like an overweight human—but demons did so less than the others. Or else Lars would have had to be seven feet tall and obese.

Lars didn't bother with human niceties like conjuring clothing. That would just waste his time. Besides, he had nothing to be ashamed of, or so he'd been assured by more than one of the ladies.

Quickly, Lars opened up the tiny pocket that held the spell components that he'd been slowly accumulating. It had been difficult but he'd managed, opening up tiny portals into the other planes and picking up ingredients. Never a handful—that would have been noticed. Instead, just a few grains here and there, always something light enough to pick up with a petite breeze spell.

All demon summoning spells were strictly human. Demons didn't summon each other. If they were well enough connected, they just had their underlings have a chat with the other demon's minions.

Chalk dust had been easy enough to bring over, along with a small bag to hold it in. Lars had been able to collect ashes the same way. The crystal had been more difficult, until he'd visited a toy shop and gotten one of those packets human children used to grow their own crystals from a powdered solution. He'd taken weeks boiling water then filtering off the excess until he had his own glowing purple crystal, imbued with magic.

The obnoxious herbs—like the damned wild oregano and rowan wood—were primarily for human protection against any demon they summoned. Lars hadn't liked handling the stuff, so there probably was something to those idiotic human myths. He'd considered discarding those parts of the incantation all together. However, Lars adamantly didn't want to *fail* again. Messing with an unfamiliar human spell seemed like a good way to do just that.

He'd also discovered that he had to be careful with the foxglove and stinging nettles. In his demon form, he might ingest them without even noticing. This damned human body was just too weak.

All the ingredients for his spell were now assembled. Carefully, Lars poured the chalk dust and ashes onto the cold dirt floor of his cell in the form of a pentacle. He placed his crystal in the space nearest him and the other ingredients in the other points of the star. Then he started his incantation.

He wasn't worried about his jailors hearing him, not when he was using his human voice, and not too loudly at that. In addition, that stupid laugh track was still playing in the background.

We'll see who gets the last laugh now.

At least human spells weren't all about endurance, unlike some of the stupid angel spells seemed to be, all that chanting that had to go on for days and days. No, humans were all about quick, fast, and efficient.

Convenient.

After about fifteen minutes of chanting, sickly yellow mist sprang up in the center of the pentagram. Lars had forgotten how badly his human body reacted to the stench of rotting flesh and nearly puked, but he made himself continue his spell.

Finally, a truly ugly demon squatted in front of Lars. It had three eyes spread across its face, all bleary and red. Its huge misshapen nose constantly dripped yellow streams of snot. Large jagged teeth filled a mouth that was too big for the rest of the face. It had three arms to match the three eyes, one disturbingly coming out of the center of its chest. All were tipped with deadly black talons meant to rip out an enemy's heart. It squatted like a toad, its bare claws digging into the dirt of the floor. When it stood up straight, it would be barely as tall as Lars in human form, though at least twice as wide.

"What's up?" the demon said. Or croaked. It had a deep bass voice that echoed in its broad chest. "Why did you summon me here?" It looked around curiously.

Lars rolled his eyes. He'd thought he'd been summoning a warrior demon. Not this scrawny thing.

He wasn't about to give up and start over, though. He could make this work.

"You're here to help me escape," Lars said honestly.

The demon looked unimpressed. "And why would I do that?" it asked reasonably enough. "There's nothing here to hold me permanently. I can just slip away."

First, Lars reached over and deliberately slapped the demon across the face, just to make it angry. Then he slid his foot forward, rubbing out the line there and breaking the pentagram.

"Why'd you do that?" the demon asked, perplexed. "Now I can just kill you for bothering me."

"That's the plan," Lars said. Then he threw back his head and howled, using his full demon voice.

"Help! I'm being attacked!"

***

It took less time than Lars expected for the guards to respond. He'd only had to slap around the frog demon about five minutes. Fortunately for him, the cell wouldn't allow either of them to cast any demon magic.

Unfortunately, Lars' human form really was more

fragile than his demon form. He had to avoid most of the clawed attacks. Damned thing could jump like a frog, and his tongue spat poison which burned Lars' human skin.

The guards did respond eventually. The door to his cell flung open and Petyr and Marty, two of the huge horse-headed guards, came striding in.

"What the hell are you doing here?" Petyr bellowed. He was the taller of the two, with red skin and broad muscles. His favorite weapon was a double-headed ax that he generally wore slung to his back. His head just about brushed the ceiling, making him between seven to eight feet tall.

Marty had his whip already in his hands and lashed out at the frog demon. He wasn't as tall or as muscled as his partner, so he tended to be a "strike first and let the gods sort out the dead souls" type of demon.

"It just appeared in my cell!" Lars exclaimed. "I think it was sent here to kill me!"

The frog-like demon stopped mid-claw to stare at Lars.

"I did not!" it bellowed. "This human conjured me here!" Then it looked for the pentagram. As they'd been fighting, Lars had carefully removed all the evidence of his spell.

"Why would I do that?" Lars asked as he edged his way closer to the door. "Why would I call a deadly demon into the room where I was trapped?"

As no one appeared to have a good answer for that, Marty lunged at the frog demon again, making it leap to the left. Petyr pivoted at the same time and slapped down the frog demon as it was sailing through the air.

"I told you that you were going to help me escape,"

Lars said to the dazed demon. "Because I'm not really a human."

Lars slipped backwards over the threshold for his cell, out of his prison and into the hallway. Instantly, his true demon form took over. It felt *unbelievably* good to be able to stretch his wings up to their full height! His tail lashed of its own accord. He couldn't belch smoke or fire, but he still worked up a good mouthful of poison and spat it at the trapped guards as he slammed the door shut in their surprised faces.

It only took Lars a few moments for him to call up a portal and get out of there, to one of the pocket worlds. He knew he didn't have much time. He'd have to make several hops to confuse the trail, so that a professional demon hunter, like Ty Brooks, wouldn't be able to track Lars' leaps.

The door to the prison that had once held Lars burst open, as he'd expected. He slashed at the guards with one hand, turning as he did so, then kicked out with one of his powerful legs. He caught the frog demon in the neck, purposefully killing it.

It wouldn't do for the frog demon to be able to testify against Lars.

Then Lars stepped through the waiting portal, into his well-deserved freedom, step one of his master plan complete.

CHAPTER TWO

SLASH. SLASH. PIVOT. DEFLECT. LEG SWIPE.

Step by step, Christine made her way through the fighting form she'd been taught by Ozlandia, the head of the king's guards.

It was kind of like human Tai Chi. Except in its troll form, it was performed with a huge double-headed ax. And a lot of growling.

Christine swung the ax over her head easily, then swept out with it, decapitating three or four imaginary attackers. She didn't really sweat as a troll. She liked to think her green-brown skin kind of glowed with the effort. The handle of the ax was big enough that Christine didn't have to worry about the claws at the ends of her fingers digging into her palm as she swung the ax around. Sharp talons also grew from the tips of her toes. It had taken some practice to learn how to walk with them and not scratch up her floors.

Her hair remained short and brown, though currently it covered her head in a mop of artificial curls. (She was never, *ever* going to get a perm again, no matter how much her human doppelganger Tina proclaimed that Christine would look cute that way.)

Christine wore a loose-fitting gray sweatshirt that she'd cut both the sleeves and the collar off of—easier to do that then to try to fix the tears that she'd accidently put in the material with her claws that one time when she'd been in a hurry. Her pants were the traditional troll variety, plain brown cotton that ended just below her knees.

She turned and slashed her ax again, first with her right hand, then with her left. The form felt good now, and she had no fear that she'd accidently let go of the ax, causing it to spin across the room and imbed itself in the far wall.

Besides, she'd only done that a few times early on.

Ozlandia had made Christine learn the full form first, testing her recall by just calling out the name of a position and having Christine be able to perform it. Only after Christine had fully memorized the form—able to perform it backwards as well as forwards—did Ozlandia take the next step, showing Christine how each position was used in combat.

At least twice a week, Christine sparred with members of the king's guard. Just as regularly, she went to one of the gyms north of the city and trained with Patrick the orc. She also practiced her form every day. It was a moving meditation for her, as the few times she'd tried doing a sitting meditation she'd promptly fallen asleep and her own snores had woken her up.

Christine had purposefully built the room she practiced in. It was located deep underground, part of the rambling home that her earth powers had helped her excavate. The ceiling was higher than the other rooms, over fourteen feet tall, so that Christine could swing her ax overhead and not have to worry about striking anything. Solid, packed earth made up the floor. The walls still contained some of the beautiful rocks *in situ* that Christine had discovered when she'd been scooping out the dirt. A string of magical lights was strung around the edges of the ceiling, glowing in bright pastel colors. They mimicked human Christmas tree lights, but were actually made out of a string of rocks that Christine had enchanted. The room smelled of good dirt, fresh and fertile, the kind that could grow anything.

Before Christine could finish going through her form, *something* announced its presence.

She came to an abrupt halt, holding her ax at the ready. What had just disturbed her?

Flinging her senses wide, Christine realized that someone on the surface had just called her name.

With merely a thought, Christine rose out of the ground and appeared at the foot of the fairy troll bridge. She'd destroyed the original bridge in order to free her air element, that aspect of her magical powers that had been bound to the stones there. Then she'd rebuilt the bridge, twice, and was now its guardian.

Christine was also the gatekeeper on this side of the bridge. While the bridge had its own powers—it wouldn't allow an oath breaker to cross it—Christine ensured that those traversing the bridge to one of the other planes didn't mean those beings harm. She also viewed herself as tour guide, and had started a collection of tourist brochures for those new to visiting the human plane.

The bridge was primarily used as the main gateway between the Pacific Northwest of the human world and Trollville. However, with the right incantation, the bridge could lead to many of the other worlds of the *kith and kin*.

"Whoa there!" came a definitely human voice as Christine swung around with her ax. "You're going to hurt someone with that thing."

Christine rolled her eyes. The voice belonged to Dennis, the human brother she'd been raised with before she'd broken the changeling spell and taken on her true troll form.

Dennis stood with a huge grin on his face, just outside of her reach. He wore an off-white wind breaker that was just a shade lighter than his beige pants. His sky-blue shirt made the blue of his eyes stand out. Cool winds gave his pale cheeks a "ruddy" quality, or so claimed Mum. He wasn't balding, not yet, but Christine could see it in the way the sandy-brown hair at the front of his head was already retreating and would leave a mere tuft in the center in just a few more years.

"You ready?" Dennis asked, sticking his hands in his jacket as yet another wind came racing down along the trees.

Though it was the start of June, it was still Seattle. The natives frequently called this time of year "Junuary." The weather was as changeable as ever, with it being sunny and in the 70s one day, then rainy and down into the 50s the next.

"Ready?" Christine asked. "For what?" She thought for

a moment. What day was it? Was it Saturday? No, she always worked Saturday mornings at the little café run by the gatekeeper on the other side of the bridge in Trollville, serving up hearty slices of ham and cheesy eggs to those who stopped by.

She'd done that yesterday, so today had to be Sunday.

Christine had problems keeping track of the days. She no longer worked her human job—needing to be on call for bridge travelers at all hours of the day and night. She'd inherited enough money to keep her comfortable, well, forever, if she didn't go crazy with it.

At least her brother no longer teased her about being "retired." Just because she no longer worked as an archivist at the library downtown didn't mean she wasn't working.

She no longer went to church with her family—she'd been haunted by too many angels to be comfortable with the human God.

However, she did still have Sunday dinner with her family on a regular basis. It wasn't time for that, was it? She glanced up. The sun was still warm and growing stronger, so it couldn't be later than eleven, at most.

Dennis sighed. "You forgot, didn't you."

"Maybe?" Christine said. It wasn't anyone's birthday— she had a reminder on her phone for those. She hadn't promised to go on another date with Dennis and his current girlfriend—the last double date had been disastrous enough that even Dennis had proclaimed his appetite for adventure had been worn thin.

"It's Father's Day," Dennis said after a bit. He looked put out. "You know, the day you spend with your family? Honoring your father? We're all going out to brunch?"

"Oh! Right!" Christine said. She remembered now. "I did get him a card and a present," she said defensively.

"Just change," Dennis said, waving his hand at her troll form. "I know you're a bad-ass princess warrior now, but we've got to go."

Christine bristled but didn't say anything. Dennis and the rest of her family sometimes forgot that the *reason* why Christine had been transforming herself into a "bad-ass princess warrior" was to protect *them*, her family.

The Great War had only been delayed. Yes, she'd put the main leader of the demons—Lars Sorgenfreys—into prison, supposedly for a century.

She didn't believe that Lars would stay there for his entire prison sentence. He'd escape, somehow. It had been five years. She had a bet with herself that he'd show up with some stupid scheme for starting up the Great War before ten years were out.

Instead of arguing with Dennis, Christine slid her ax into its holder on her back, then touched the amulet hanging around her neck on a silver chain. She didn't actually need the amulet in order to transform from her true troll self to her human form. She used it more as a focusing point.

The amulet contained a pretty blue stone set in swirling silver wire. Christine had been drawn to it because of the asymmetry of the piece, how the wire looped from the top left side to the bottom right. It wasn't until much later that she realized that the amulet actually resembled the royal troll sigil, her personal symbol that was tied to much of her magic.

Originally, the amulet had contained a transformation

spell. Christine had accidently burned it out before she'd realized her own magical powers.

Christine didn't physically transform, like a demon or a shape shifter. She didn't merely cast an illusion spell either. What she did was somewhere in between, her troll self shrinking down to human size, following the conservation of mass so she appeared as a very curvy human female. Then an illusion spell wrapped her skin, changing it from the dark green-brown of a troll to a lighter human color. Though the rest of her family had the pale white and ruddy complexions of the British, Christine had always thought of herself as being more Mediterranean colored. It was just one of the ways she differed from her human family.

Her hair stayed the unruly dark brown mop, but her jaw shortened to human dimensions, her upper and lower fangs withdrawing. Instead of the old sweatshirt and half pants, Christine dressed herself in a nice white blouse and jeans.

Christine knew that while a human male might think of her as "cute," most wouldn't even take a second look at her. Which was fine by her, now that she realized she was a troll and actually only attracted to male trolls. (She was officially a millennial, who tended to not put a lot of focus on the gender of their partners. Christine had learned that it was only male trolls who she was attracted to, though she always held herself open to the possibility that she just hadn't met the right female yet.)

After Christine finished her transformation, she turned and put a low-level shield spell across the bridge. It was kind of like turning the "Open" sign in a shop over to the

"Closed" side. If anyone had serious need, the bridge would allow them to cross anyway. However, most travelers would wait until Christine returned.

"You need to put these things in your calendar or something," Dennis said, still intent on scolding her.

Christine shrugged. While her human family meant the world to her, the rest of the human holidays didn't hold as much meaning as they once had. She would come to Christmas, but she first celebrated the coming of the light with her troll relatives.

It was kind of like being adopted into a family with a different religion.

Christine had tried bringing Alan, which was short for Alanorin, along to some of her family get togethers. But he was much more trollish than she was, having been raised in Trollville. He was uncomfortable here in the human plane, as most trolls were. It was one of the reasons why Christine had met so few trolls in Seattle, the bridge troll in Fremont notwithstanding.

"Anyway, I'm glad I got a chance to talk with you before we got there," Dennis said as they got into his car. It was the same car that he'd driven for years. Christine always got a tiny thrill out of the small burned mark in the ceiling from one of the first times she'd actually performed magic.

"Okay," Christine said. She could have gotten herself to her parent's condo down in Madison Park through one of the portals. There was one in the Japanese garden just across the street from the bridge, and another one down on the docks half a block from her parent's building. However, she'd discovered that while she could bring

Dennis or other mundanes through them, it took a lot of focus and energy.

As much as Dennis had tried, it turned out he had no magic whatsoever, something that Christine suspected still irked him.

Dennis pulled onto Madison Street before he continued. "Do you think that some of that, you know, thing that had infected Dad, is still there?"

"What do you mean?" Christine said. "What makes you ask that?"

"He's starting to act kind of funny," Dennis said. "And forgetful."

"Dad's always been kind of funny, you know," Christine said. He used words like "swell" and "golly gee"—not because he was old enough to have used them as a kid, but because he thought it was cool. He'd semi-retired the month before, cutting down his work to just three days a week, Tuesday through Thursday.

"Yeah, but…he seems to be growing more funny," Dennis said. "And his memory is getting really bad."

That worried Christine. "He isn't coming down with something like Alzheimer's, is he?" Trolls didn't tend to get those sorts of human illnesses, including heart attacks or cancer.

Dennis shrugged. He still looked worried. "I don't know. But is there something you can do? Can you take him to a healer or something?"

It was Christine's turn to shrug. "I'll talk to Nik about it," she promised. While she knew that there were some troll healers, they specialized in fixing broken limbs and sewing up battle wounds. Plus, there were very few trolls who actually had magic, and they tended to be in the royal family. Healers had their own guilds and families, and didn't traditionally have magic.

"And I'll ask Tina," Christine added after a moment.

Tina was Christine's human doppelganger. Tina was actually Christine's parents' biological daughter. Christine and Tina had been swapped at birth so that Tina could be raised in a magical family and fulfill her Destiny.

Tina was the most magical person Christine knew. She actually *glowed* when she got excited talking about magic. It had taken a few years of convincing, but Tina was finally over the fact that it appeared that Christine had usurped her Destiny when she'd broken the changeling spell.

"Thanks for checking," Dennis said.

They were quiet the rest of the way down the hill to the lake, silent in their worry.

It seemed so unfair to Christine. She was doing everything in her power to protect her family from external threats.

How could she protect them from internal threats like human disease?

CHAPTER THREE

Nikolai waited patiently behind his counter for the next customer to come to Nik's Emporium and Trade Goods. He was good at waiting. It was an art that he'd practiced over the centuries.

Waiting for the next customer. Waiting for shipments of specially ordered spell components. Waiting for the next Great War.

The shop was as tidy as Nik was willing to keep it. Magic kept the gray tile floor swept clean—one of the first tasks he'd "automated." Wooden shelves—many of them built by him—filled the open floor. The ceiling rose up over eighteen feet tall, so that the giants who came to shop didn't have to crouch over. Magic also kept cobwebs from forming up there.

Human light fixtures holding long neon light tubes ran along the ceiling. They weren't powered by electricity, but by magic. They automatically adjusted themselves to the brightness that a customer required. Colorful posters advertising various goods lined the walls. Nik found it particularly amusing that some of the companies now used human actors representing those well-known elves and dwarves from the movies, though real elves and dwarves didn't look anything like the Hollywood portrayals.

Nik took a lot of care to make sure that the room generally smelled "neutral." A lot of spell components came with strong scents—like the dried chicken feet or the green mushrooms—that would attract only a small percentage of his clientele. Still, he frequently detected a sweet Frankincense fragrance floating through the air.

Though Nik told his customers that he'd been around since the last Great War, that was only technically true. He had run the same magical emporium then as now, located in a small pocket between worlds. (Though he had to admit he much preferred the current incarnation—running his shop out of a tent had always been difficult. Particularly when it came to keeping the flies out of the ointments.)

Before the previous war, over two thousand years ago, he'd been one of the strongest human magicians around, though few would have realized it. Nikolai had always maintained a low profile. However, he'd learned the hard way that a human body was too easily compromised. Not only physically, but mentally.

Demons had influenced Nik's actions without him even realizing it. He'd never forgiven himself for how he'd betrayed humanity, even though, strictly speaking, it hadn't been his fault.

When the Great War had ended and the humans had won, an angel who'd owed Nik a favor had helped him transfer his consciousness over to the wooden body he'd built.

Nik had wanted to create a much taller version of himself. That hadn't been possible though, not with the technology of that time. He'd come to accept that he would spend eternity being just three feet tall. He wore a charm that cast the illusion that his painted mouth spoke, and that his painted eyes held the entire range of human emotions.

From the looks Christine shot him from time to time, he wondered if it was time to renew those charms.

Today he wore his usual modern clothing—brightly colored plaid shirt, today in baby blue, sunset red, white and black—along with a comfortable pair of loose-fitting slacks. Black leather shoes covered his wooden feet, hiding the fact that he'd never quite perfected the joints of his toes.

Christine should be arriving soon. She came to the shop every other week and catalogued his various finds. Nik specialized in antiques and frequently went to auctions and estate sales. Not the human variety, but either from a demon who'd just passed or one of the *kith and kin*. The heirs usually just boxed everything up and sold it, not bothering to assess the treasures they had.

While finding potential treasure was important, Nik's true super power (as he liked to think of it in this modern age) lay in knowing *exactly* who needed what he'd discovered. Particularly since the internet did *not* run outside of the human realm, something Nik was sure was the Host's meddling.

A quiet ping rang through the shop. To all but Nik, it

would have been imperceptible. It meant that someone had activated the portal in one of the planes and was on their way here.

Nik put a pleased expression on his face, anticipating Christine.

However, Lars Sorgenfreys walked into the shop. Nik recognized his human form—handsome overall but with a smarmy smile and blond hair that still fell into his blue eyes, giving him that bad boy vibe. He'd not aged much during his time in prison.

"How can I help you?" Nik called out as Lars stayed by the entrance, still looking around, as if waiting for a hidden threat.

"You're still neutral, right?" Lars said finally as he strode across the shop, stalking toward Nik.

"I am," Nik said proudly. It had been one of the promises he'd had to make to the angel who'd helped him transfer his consciousness. As long as he remained neutral and sold goods to all sides, he was assured almost eternal life.

He was fairly certain that only his mind had been moved from one body to the other. His soul had probably stayed behind. That was the only reason he could think of for the hollow feeling he sometimes got. However, that lack of moral conscience also helped him remain truly neutral, even when his heart may have directed his hand to help the humans now and again.

"You sure?" Lars inquired. "I heard you turned in an account book you'd found."

Nik nodded. Many of his demon customers had had the same question. It hadn't been great for business.

However, despite his lack of soul he knew that he'd done the right thing. Keeping an accounting book that a demon had used for tracking the souls he'd acquired would have tainted Nik. Plus, it had shown how the court had been corrupted by demons—yet another entity that was supposed to stay neutral.

"I couldn't have contained the book," Nik explained. "The evil magic would have leaked."

Lars nodded, satisfied with that explanation, as most of the demons were. Of course, their magic was too strong for someone like Nik.

"You wouldn't have seen that meddlesome troll recently, have you?" Lars inquired. He leaned across the counter. "Christine?"

Was he doing that to bring his head lower to Nik's? Probably not. He was probably thinking that by coming closer he could intimidate Nik.

Youngster certainly had a lot to learn.

Nik deliberately gave a carefree laugh.

Interesting. Lars' entire body shuddered at that.

"Don't know the meaning of the word neutral, do you?" Nik countered. "That means selling goods to all the races. It also means not reporting on the movements of any individuals."

For a moment, it felt to Nik as though an ant crawled across the back of his neck. He banished the sensation easily.

"Now, try to influence me again in order to get your way is one of the quickest ways to get yourself barred from here," Nik growled.

It was curious, however, that the demon's work had

been that strong. Frequently, the sensation of someone trying to influence him was so slight he didn't notice.

"Sorry! Sorry!" Lars said, leaning back up, spreading his hands out as if he was the most innocent being alive. "But you can't blame me for trying."

"Yes, I can," Nik said coldly. "What do you want."

Lars reeled off a list of ingredients.

Nik gave a low whistle. "Don't have all of those in stock," he said after thinking for a moment. "It will take a couple weeks to get the hog's breath."

Lars looked put out, but he merely nodded and said, "Fine. Let me know when they all come in."

He was about to sweep out of the shop, make some grand exit, but Nik put the kibosh on that. He reached across the counter and laid a single finger on Lars' arm, holding him in place.

Nik was surprised at how normal the demon's human flesh felt, not burning up with the fires of Hell or freezing with ice either. Not that Nik made a habit of touching anyone. He'd learned the trick of focusing a customer's attention when it was necessary.

"Payment first," Nik said as he lifted his finger.

Lars' eyes narrowed. "Half," he said.

Nik shrugged. "There's no demand for three-fourths of the list you just gave me. I can't get the item in and then have you change your mind. No one else I could sell it to. Full payment, for everything, up front."

Lars gave Nik a cool smile and settled into a serious bargaining mode.

What little joy Nik felt came from times like these.

These modern youngsters were far too used to being ripped off with fixed prices.

However, Nik didn't allow the bargaining to go on as long as he normally would have.

He needed Lars out of there before Christine arrived.

Even he might not be able to prevent the war that would erupt between them.

NIK LOOKED UP AND NODDED AT CHRISTINE WHEN she finally entered the shop. He wasn't sure why she was so late that day—though he was certain that she'd tell him, probably in excruciating detail, so unlike a troll. She'd picked up many human habits as she'd been raised by them.

Would she ever outgrow them? Possibly. If she lived that long.

But Nik couldn't think about that.

He kept his attention on the brownie who was currently trying to bargain him down on the price of a pack of strong steel awls, used to puncture leather. Seemed that a recent brawl between the young man he was serving and the young man's wife had caused her to throw his into the hearth.

Nik practiced patience as the young brownie fretted over the cost. Nik pointed out to him, again, that these were an investment in not just his future, but his family's future.

Besides, how thrilled would his wife be with a new pair of custom, handmade shoes?

After getting a much better price than he'd expected, Nik joined Christine in the back room of the shop. A thick, purple velvet curtain separated the two rooms, enchanted, of course, to keep the noise and smells of the two rooms apart.

Tall metal shelves filled the walls back here, industrial racks Nik had bought for a song. They were neutral, being human made. It would take an actual spell for them to pick up any magical residue. (The wooden shelves that Nik had made had the same quality.) Boxes lined the shelves, all duly numbered and accounted for. They'd come from an estate he'd acquired forty years ago.

He'd never admitted to Christine that he had three—no, four—warehouses stacked to the gills with boxes, though he knew she suspected as much. He couldn't help it. He really liked buying full estates, just so he would have the right thing when a customer came along.

Nik trusted that his magical sense would lead him to the exact box containing the exact right item that a customer needed. However, when the boxes were already inventoried, his magical sense took a lot less time.

It wasn't that Nik needed the money. He didn't eat. He rarely slept, though he did occasionally "shut down," as he liked to think of it, became unaware of his surroundings for a period of time, at least once a month. But only when he was completely alone. He woke up instantly when a customer came through the portal.

The shop was expensive to run, between all the ingredients needed for the various spells, as well as the bribes he paid to various gatekeepers to keep access to the shop open for all.

Nik just liked having so much gold stashed away, a metal that all the races valued. He knew that it wouldn't make up for the soul he'd lost. It still assuaged the hollowness sometimes.

"What do you think?" Nik asked as he came in the backroom where Christine was waiting.

Christine carefully lifted another large box down from the top shelf. "I think," she said, pausing as she blew a layer of dust from the box, "that you've been holding these for quite some time." She sneezed suddenly and shook her head.

"Maybe," Nik said. He liked to play coy with Christine, making her guess the actual age of the estate based on the contents. She was getting much better at it.

Since Christine had been raised as a human, she lacked the general cultural knowledge about the *kith and kin* and the other races that she would have picked up normally, just absorbed as part of her growing up.

When they'd started out, Nik had put strong magical protection around all the boxes he brought into the store so that Christine wouldn't open one without him in the room. It wasn't that he didn't trust her, but that he needed to make sure that he could contain any magical booby traps that she might accidently set off.

Not that Christine's tough troll body couldn't absorb an awful lot of magical as well as physical damage.

Over the years Christine had figured out how to avoid being blown up, even when Nik wasn't there to supervise. Before, asking her to come and talk with him when she ran across something unusual would have meant that she stopped at almost every item. Now, she had enough magical training to be able to detect something before it reached out and bit her.

"So, you have forty-one boxes," Christine commented, carefully filling out the spreadsheet she'd developed for keeping track of inventory. "It's going to take me a couple weekends to go through each one," she warned before she opened the first box.

"I figured that," Nik said. "Take all the time you want."

He'd be sure to call Lars back to the shop on a day when Christine wasn't coming.

Christine opened the first box and pulled out what looked like a cheap human lamp. The base of the lamp had been made out of porcelain in the form of a hula dancer, complete with a grass skirt and coconut-shell covered breasts. However, it had been enchanted, as Christine discovered when she pressed the button that turned the lamp on.

The girl started dancing slowly, swaying her hips from side to side. A golden light emanated from the bamboo lampshade. Soft Hawaiian music filled the background.

Christine snorted and put the lamp down. "This have a name besides 'tacky demon shit'?"

Nik grinned. "What, don't you think your brother would love such a lamp?"

"Maybe," Christine said. "I'll have to see if you still have it when his birthday rolls around." She paused then turned to Nik. "Can I ask you a question?"

"Sure," Nik said, surprised that she hadn't just come out and demanded an answer as soon as she'd walked in.

Trolls didn't tend to be patient, and Christine's human upbringing hadn't affected that much.

"You remember five years ago when I brought my dad here? And you removed that spike of influence from him that had originally infected Dennis?" Christine said.

Nik nodded solemnly. He'd been so glad that Christine had brought her father to him as quickly as she had. Not many other magicians would have been capable of removing that demon spike. It had twined its way through the lungs of the man's body. If she had waited just another week, Nik may not have been able to remove it without damage.

"Is there any chance that some sliver of it remained?" Christine asked. "Now, I didn't see it," she continued quickly, "but Dennis swears that Dad is acting funny. Funnier than usual. And he's become more forgetful, too."

"No, none of it remained," Nik said. "I removed all of it. And I gave your dad, I guess what you'd call a booster shot too, something to inoculate him from demon influence. It isn't foolproof. He could still be influenced. But you have protections set up at your parents' house, right?"

Christine nodded. "And amulets for them to wear. When they remember to wear them." She rolled her eyes. "I just can't convince them that the threat's real. It's been five years. It's like they don't remember."

"They don't," Nik said softly. "You're the only one who's fought a demon. More than once. You won't ever forget almost losing your life. They didn't fight. They weren't physically hurt by a demon. They're human. Their memories are supposed to wear thin after a while." Nik had always considered that a design flaw. It was part of the reason why he'd switched bodies.

Christine sighed and nodded. "I supposed you're right. Dennis remembers. But he was also attacked, once. And infected. He always wears the bracelet I created for him and never takes it off. He was dating a woman once who didn't like it. Took it as a sign to break up with her."

"That's smart," Nik said. He had tried to teach the young man some of the basics of magic, but nothing had stuck. He was mundane. Nothing magical about him.

Human magic tended to run in families. However, besides Tina, there didn't seem to be anyone else in the Tuckerman family who had magic. Christine had made an effort to reconnect with all her human relatives on her dad's side at least once over the past five years, but they were all mundane, at least as far as she could tell.

Tina had to have come from somewhere. Nik wondered if it was from one of Christine's British relatives whom she'd never met, as her mum had been raised in the UK.

"Do you know of any healer who could help my dad? And his memory?" Christine asked as she turned back to the box. "If, you know, there's actually anything wrong?"

"No," Nik said. "It doesn't work that way." Magical healing could be used on a mundane human who'd been hurt, particularly if they'd been physically damaged by something magical. But it didn't work great. Nik had a theory that magic needed magic to call to itself, so that any magical healing could go further than skin deep.

"Okay," Christine said, nodding. She pulled out the next item. It was about a foot long and half that wide.

Each end had a hinged piece of wood, about three inches square, that folded down.

Christine held the piece up, joy in her voice. "An antique book holder!" she exclaimed. Then she frowned. "There's a trace of magic in it."

She put the book holder on the ground then unfolded the two ends.

A faint illusion of a collection of books sprang up, filling the holder from one end to the other.

Nik peered over Christine's shoulder. The titles were all written in one of the more obscure demon languages.

"What, was this so that the demon could impress whoever he'd brought home for the evening?" Christine asked.

"Maybe," Nik said slowly. He paused, then pointed to a box that was on the middle shelf, with two other boxes on top of it. "Can you fetch that one, please?"

Christine walked over to the shelf and easily lifted down the boxes on top of the box Nik wanted.

Nik just shook his head. He forgot just how strong Christine was. Of course, Nik could have performed the same task with magic. And his wooden joints were well supported. But he still would have had problems, not just because of his size but because those particular boxes had been heavy.

Even Christine wasn't strong enough to hold both boxes up with a single hand. She fetched the box Nik had felt was right, putting the others back on the shelf. Before she opened it, she added the number of the box into her inventory.

This was why Nik needed Christine. He would have

just opened the box, and then gotten hopelessly mixed up in the inventory of items, placing the things he found in one box into the other and vice versa.

It was odd for a troll to be so precise. Nik had always figured it was because of the changeling spell that had tied Christine's entire personality to Tina's, so that Christine developed the same tastes and habits as the human.

Books filled the box Christine had lifted down. Nik didn't have to see her face to know how her eyes had just lit up.

"Match them up," Nik instructed.

He knew that Christine couldn't read the titles. She'd learned Trollish because that was her native language, and had picked up some words in the common demon form, as well as a few of the other languages. It had frustrated her to no end that while she adored books and reading, languages didn't come easily to her.

It took Christine a while to find the right books that went on the small book holder. There had been thirteen in all. When she finished and slid the last book into place, all of the physical books vanished, as Nik had been expecting.

"Wow," Christine said, obviously not expecting that. "What just happened?"

"Fold down the ends, then open them again," Nik instructed.

Christine did as she'd been instructed. The physical books reappeared.

"It's a way of protecting magical texts," Nik said. "With the right incantation, the book holder will empty again."

"Cool," Christine said. "I didn't think demons were

into writing down magical incantations. Can I look at one?"

"Sure."

Christine lifted one of the texts and opened it. The pages were full of drawings as well as texts. She looked through a few pages then glanced up at Nik. "It isn't spells, is it?"

"It isn't. It's a brag shelf." He looked over her shoulder. "These books detail the battles, real as well as made-up, that this demon's ancestors or family fought over the centuries. So it's a kind of family history."

"Huh," Christine said as she put the book back. "How do you want it inventoried? With the books, or without?"

They came up with a cross-referencing system and Christine moved onto the next item while Nik went out to wait on the next customer.

He hadn't admitted to Christine just how rare that book holder and collection was. Demons tended to exaggerate their successes while minimizing or denying their failures.

Yet, the book he'd glanced at detailed not only this demon's wins, but his losses as well.

It would give the right opponent to the demons a leg up, giving them some valuable information for how to beat this type of demon.

Nik would have to think long and hard about who should be notified about these books.

Because while he was strictly neutral and sold ingredients to all the races, that didn't mean he didn't sometimes favor the humans.

CHAPTER FOUR

Tina sighed as she put her wand down on the floor beside her. It was long and wooden, kind of like those wands from the popular movies. However, hers really worked.

Most of the time.

Tina fought down a spike of panic. She was *not* losing her magic. She was just having a bad morning. She was not going to count having a similar bad day last week—she'd just been tired that afternoon. Or the week before, after that blowup with her roommate.

She couldn't lose her magic on top of losing her Destiny and everything else.

After taking a few deep breaths and rolling her shoulders, Tina was able to force herself to relax. She pulled her pretty pink T-shirt down and spread her fingers wide across her jean-covered thighs. Though her mentors had always disapproved, Tina frequently did magic barefoot. She'd let her blonde hair grow out this past year, and held it back in a cute pony tail.

Tina wasn't wearing any makeup that day—she generally only put on "full war paint" when she was going out at night. Besides, she was aware that she really didn't need it. She had a beautiful peaches and cream complexion with small pores, her lips were naturally pink, her cheeks always had color in them, and her eyes were a searing blue.

A thought came to her. She'd had a fight with Nicky, her girlfriend, the night before. *That* must be what was distracting Tina today, why her magic was being flaky.

Not because she was inexplicably growing weaker magically.

Tina sat cross legged on the floor of her magical practice room. The room was only about ten feet by ten feet, cozy enough for her to feel warm there, yet also spacious enough so that she didn't feel cramped. The room didn't exist on the human plane. Tina and her mentor at the time had carved it out of a space between the worlds.

She'd colored the walls a pale, restful, green, then applied a beautiful swirling white pattern across them, like tendrils of wind blowing across a field of grass. She frequently brought in the smell of summer, of freshly mowed lawns with a trace of cool mountain air.

Soft mats covered the floor, so it was always comfortable enough to either stand or sit for hours. Nothing lined the walls. Tina had created many small pockets of space where she stashed her magical implements. It was one of the spells that came naturally to her.

According to her parents, or rather, the people who'd adopted and raised her, she'd started creating those pockets before she could talk, hiding her stuffed animals to keep them safe.

The Zimmermans had never liked the idea of Tina practicing so far away. They'd been worried that she'd blow herself up.

Okay, so that had only happened the one time.

However, Tina had put a set of protection spells on a timer. If she didn't return to the human plane after a specific amount of time, the practice room would turn itself inside out and dump her back in the room that she'd grown up in.

It meant that her adoptive parents could never sell their house. Or she'd just show up in a stranger's house. She could redo the spells, and she would someday when she bought her own house. For now, she lived in a shared townhouse. It kept the cost of rent down and gave her some necessary freedom from her adoptive parents, though she still made sure to have dinner with them once a week.

That had been something else her adoptive parents hadn't liked. They'd hidden her away for most of her life in an effort to keep her safe. The oracles had proclaimed that Tina had a Destiny and was supposed to lead armies in the Great War.

So the Zimmermans had adopted Christine when she'd been a troll baby. They'd turned her into a changeling, an exact human replica of Tina. Then they'd stolen Tina from her biological parents, replacing her with Christine, and raised Tina as their own daughter, so that she could achieve her full magical potential.

The old witch who'd cast the changeling spell claimed

that she'd been visited by a being of light who'd somehow twined or joined Tina's Destiny with Christine's.

Now, the Oracles saw no clear future for Tina. They couldn't even say if Tina still had a Destiny or not.

It had taken Tina a lot of time and effort (and some costly therapy) to get over the fact that she might not be the most special human magician of all time, that her adoptive parent's expectations—and her teachers' and everyone else's—might no longer be valid.

Tina was still an incredibly strong human magician. No lack of prophecy could take that away from her. Despite how wonky her magic had grown the last few weeks.

She just might no longer have a major place in the grand scheme of things.

And she was okay with that. Now. Most days.

Today had just been a bad day. She felt, well, magically constipated might be a good term. She couldn't seem to get even the simplest of spells right. Everything felt difficult, as if her arms were weighed down with rocks and her mouth jammed up with gum.

It should have been easy to scry on one of her old tutors, Malcom. He had always been so friendly and kind, reminding her of Mr. Rogers, though he didn't physically resemble the man at all. Malcom was African American, tall and stately, with an easy smile and closely cropped hair that had just started going gray along the temples.

Malcom had taught Tina the fundamentals of magic. All magic was like learning music. While there was a lot that she could discover on her own, if she really wanted to learn how to play the piano, she needed to learn from someone else who could play and who could teach her proper technique.

Tina had grown past Malcom rather quickly, staying with him for barely a year. However, he'd continued to check in on her, always making himself available for questions or just a shoulder to cry on.

Malcom had adequate protections to keep his home safe from demons. But he'd never barred her from entry before.

Was it just her? Or had he decided he didn't want anyone peeking in?

Tina picked up her wand and tried casting the scrying spell again. She didn't need any ingredients for the spell. It should have been simple enough.

But it just…fizzled. She couldn't think of any other term for it.

Tina felt the power build up, focused and certain. It was like holding a bubbling pot, getting ready to aim the accumulated steam. She had the right location in mind, Malcom's living room. (She wouldn't observe him in his study. That was a private place for all magicians, and she respected that.) However, when she tried to tunnel out of her practice room and into the human plane, all her power and focus dissipated. It was like she was shooting a tiny flame into a powerful wall of water.

Was it just Malcom? Or was it her scrying powers? Could she scry on someone else?

Tina didn't try looking in on Christine. Her troll defenses had grown stronger over the years. Plus, Christine wouldn't have liked Tina spying on her.

How about Dennis, Christine's brother? He was

strictly mundane, no magical powers whatsoever. Tina hadn't been able to teach him the simplest spells, and neither had Nik.

It was a shame, as Tina would have liked to have a student someday. She wasn't likely to ever have any kids, particularly not with Nicky. Though maybe if they got married, they could adopt…

That was part of the problem, however.

Nicky was out, loud and proud.

Tina…wasn't.

She'd told her bio parents, the Tuckermans. They'd been perfectly fine with their biological daughter being gay. Then again, they'd had to accept that the daughter who they'd thought was theirs had actually turned out to be a troll.

Her adoptive parents, the Zimmermans, had been more difficult. Tina had come out to them and told them that she was a lesbian. However, they'd blamed the changeling spell for her preference.

While Tina found their logic convoluted, she hadn't been able to get them to change their minds.

Christine only liked trolls. She didn't find humans attractive in the least. While that was a tendency for most trolls, Tina had heard of at least one human-troll couple who'd made it work for at least a few decades.

Therefore, at least according to her adoptive parents, if Christine only liked "the same," that is, trolls, then Tina liking "the same," that is, girls, must be the result of the spell, not Tina's actual orientation.

Nicky understood that Tina's adoptive parents had

issues with her coming out, and so had never pushed to go over there and meet them.

However, she didn't understand why Tina hadn't bothered coming out to anyone else.

For Tina, it struck her that it was nobody's goddamned business who or what she slept with, as long as it was all consensual.

It also meant that Tina had told Nicky that she wasn't going to accompany Nicky to the Seattle Pride parade later that month.

Tina didn't like loud parties or large groups of people. Going to the Pride Party up on Capitol Hill with ten thousand of her "closest friends" sounded like Hell, quite frankly.

Nicky had claimed that it was important, particularly given the current social and government climate. That Tina needed to show her support.

Tina wanted to do that in other ways, not by spending a day being hemmed in on all sides by drunken party-goers.

It was why she'd wanted to look in on Malcom, to breathe in some of his calm. But obviously, that wasn't happening today.

Tina thought back to Dennis Tuckerman. She'd been to his house a few times, as well as ridden in his car. He was a regular human though, and probably wasn't home. It was Monday, and he'd probably be at his office downtown, a place she'd never been before.

However, Tina had frequently been to the Tuckermans' house. And she knew that just this last month, Mr. Tuckerman—Vern—had changed to part-time employment, only working three days a week at the insurance firm. He would be home today.

Maybe she should look in on him instead.

It took Tina a few seconds to focus in on the Tuckermans' house. She loved the open floor plan of the main room and kitchen. The front windows overlooked Lake Washington, and got a lot of glorious sunshine in the mornings.

This time, Tina's scrying spell went straight through to the house of the Tuckermans. She found she had a ceiling view of the living room. Mr. Tuckerman sat at his desk against the far wall, putting together one of his remote-control airplanes. He built them from scratch out of balsa wood. He had a pattern that he followed, and he cut out each piece by hand. It took incredible patience. Then he had to assemble the plane, attach the struts to the main wings, create the hollowed-out fuselage, run all the important wires.

Sunlight came streaming through the windows to the right of his desk. Mrs. Tuckerman wasn't in the room— she was either out someplace (as she was much more social than he was) or she was just out of view in the kitchen. Or maybe she was at her work.

Before Tina could move her focus and find out, Mr. Tuckerman straightened up in his seat, seeming wary, as if he'd heard an unfamiliar noise.

Slowly, he turned and stared straight at the spot on the wall from which Tina was viewing the room.

Could he see her? That wasn't possible, was it? He didn't have any magic.

Yet, he stared right at her. Hard.

He rose from his seat, walking directly toward her. What was he doing? What did he think he saw?

Up close, Tina saw the tiredness that was creeping in around Mr. Tuckerman's handsome face. He looked older this close up. He had the blue eyes of the rest of the family and sandy blond hair. He had a long face with a large nose, something that Tina had thankfully not inherited. She looked more like her biological mother, with softer features.

Mr. Tuckerman raised his hand, then with his thumb, pressed firmly against the exact spot that Tina was looking out from, like he was killing a bug on the wall.

With a soft *pop*, Tina's spell was broken.

That wasn't supposed to happen at all.

Either Tina's magic really was growing weak, or someone in Tina's biological family did have magic.

Her bio dad.

CHAPTER FIVE

THE CURRENT INCARNATION OF BEELZEBUB (KNOWN as Buddy to his friends) sat on his throne and listened to the plans Lars Sorgenfreys was so excited about. The throne room held just the pair of them, as Lars had requested a private audience. And his family had been willing to pay the "fee" that Buddy had asked for, guaranteeing his undivided attention.

Buddy scratched his bare belly and belched as Lars went on and on and *on*. A trail of smoke rose up from Buddy's fanged mouth. Too many chilies in the salsa that Buddy had had with his burrito that morning.

The throne room really could use some spiffing up. The glowing red rock and fire motif was kind of done, you know? Maybe Buddy should go really retro and do a whole steel/industrial dungeon look. The room was big enough to hold two dozen horse-sized demons, with the ceilings tall enough for them to all stand up and not have to bow their heads.

Demons tended to be against any sort of bowing.

Which Buddy understood. One of his first incarnations had been insistent about that, particularly with the whole human-Morningstar mess.

Lars' enthusiasm appeared to be running down.

"So what do you need from me?" Buddy asked. May as well get to the chase. Lars wasn't there to spend the morning chatting about the (awful) state of the worlds.

Lars looked with disdain down the long ridge of his nose. Sure, his wings were kind of impressive, made out of boney struts with what looked like ripped black leather hanging in tatters from them. His eyes had that flayed flesh look that had become so popular a few years back. Black poison dripped from his tongue—part of the reason why all the rooms in Buddy's palace had magically-reinforced stone floors, though they still needed regular maintenance.

"I need four armies," Lars said. "As I explained. I need them sent to various worlds of the *kith and kin*. They won't really be in danger, not until the war actually starts. They're the primary distraction."

"And why should I help you and not just send your ass back to prison?" Buddy asked reasonably. He stood up from the throne made of iron casts of the skulls of his enemies and stretched.

Sure, Buddy didn't usually appear very threatening. He had a large floppy nose, flabby lips, as much hair sprouting from the moles on his face and chest as on his skull. His potbelly rumbled and the gas that escaped was truly noxious. (Seriously. He'd done the experiments. It could kill a human in the right conditions.)

He generally went around barefoot, without a shirt,

wearing just a pair of old stained Bermuda shorts that hung down to just over his knees. (Took a closer look to realize it really was blood that Buddy had spilled down the side of the shorts. Or a keen nose.)

Buddy didn't need to look like one of the princes of Hell to actually *be*, well, a prince from Hell. He had the tenure and the guts to do what needed doing.

Other demons tended to underestimate him, something Buddy used to his advantage. Ruthlessly. They all seemed to forget just how old he *actually* was, and how their power games were junior varsity compared to the big players.

Lars' attitude seemed to be somewhere between exasperated and cautious.

Good enough.

Lars seemed to be thinking about the question that Buddy posed to him for a great while.

"Out with it," Buddy growled. He'd guaranteed Lars an hour. And that time was almost up, at least as far as Buddy was concerned.

"Why should you help me? Because I can ensure that we win the war," Lars said.

"How?" Buddy asked. That was the meat of issue. It wasn't that demons were lazy—okay, well, maybe they were—but they really, *really* hated losing. It was why the Great War kept getting put off. No one could guarantee a win.

And really, why bother declaring all-out war if there was no guarantee?

Lars sighed. "I'll show you. But no one else knows all the details."

Buddy made a circling motion for Lars to just get on with it. The youngster certainly liked the sound of his own voice.

Lars made a scooping motion with his hand off to the side, then turned his palm up to show Buddy.

Interesting! Storing materials in pockets of space was a human thing. Demons didn't need such trivial magic. They either carried their own gear with them, or had minions to fetch it for them.

A pile of what looked like small diamonds glittered in the center of Lars' palm. Each had its own glow, though together they were quite bright.

"What are those?" Buddy asked. He didn't reach for one. Just one damned booby trapped "gift" from Zelinius had cured Buddy of that tendency quickly.

"Corruptions spells," Lars said. He couldn't smile with that snout of his. He still gave off the feeling of smug satisfaction. "Corrupted."

"Explain yourself," Buddy said, sitting back down on his throne. It wasn't that he wanted to get away from that damaged, cracked set of crystals. He was both attracted to them and repelled by them at the same time.

"When a demon ingests one of these, their ability to influence humans goes off the charts," Lars ensured Buddy.

"Ingests?" Buddy growled. Who the fuck was Lars kidding? Had he not thought this brilliant plan through? Hell, Buddy's own minions might disobey a direct order about swallowing.

"Merely carrying one will work too," Lars said hastily.

"Though it's only by ingesting that you'll get the full benefit."

"For how long?" Buddy asked, bravely reaching for one.

Lars froze for a moment before he gracefully reached out his hand. As close to graceful as a hand primarily composed of bones and long poisonous talons could move.

"I estimate up to three years," Lars said.

Buddy held the crystal up to his eyes, looking through it. It was, as Lars said, a corruption spell that had been corrupted. A normal corruption spell worked quickly, spreading disease, filth, and a lack of morals in a matter of moments, like a tsunami from Hell.

Ah, the good old days, when Buddy could command his armies to rape, pillage, and corrupt at will.

This crystal though, it held what humans would call a time-released capsule of corruption. Instead of the filth piling up in the corners of a cursed house in a matter of weeks, it would take years.

"So how does this help spread a demon's influence?" Buddy growled. He was confused, and he didn't like it.

"First of all, because the work is so slow, the humans don't have any counter measures," Lars said proudly. "My family has been secreting these in key locations for years, now."

"Still haven't explained why I should help you," Buddy said. His patience was just about at an end. And Buddy considered himself a patient guy.

"Using one of these, a demon's influence also increases in the short term," Lars said hastily. "Imagine, an entire army whose mere presence starts the onslaught of fear, uncertainty, and doubt. Then the generals start the serious spells. Because the corrupted corruption spell has already softened the target, more of the other spells get through. When battle is joined, it's just a mop up job for the boys."

Buddy nodded. These things could really do the trick.

That didn't detract from the fact that Lars was still an idiot.

"Suppose I give you the four armies," Buddy said slowly. "I'm assuming you'll outfit them, feed them, direct them?"

Lars didn't really have much of a throat, but he still gulped before he nodded.

Outfitting and feeding a demon army was expensive. No matter how good the accountant you hired to keep track of all the money, you were still going to pay through the nose for some things, be cheated on the rest.

They were demons doing business with primarily other demons, after all.

That would take a bunch of creatures off Buddy's hands for a while. He might even make a profit on this if he handled it correctly, insisting that Lars used only the vendors of Buddy's choice when it came to weapons, armor and such.

"And with the special fairy magic crystals, you think you can win," Buddy said, flipping the crystal back to Lars.

The boy bit his tongue and didn't reply to the insult, which was a good thing. But he did nod, then say, "Yes. Yes, I'm certain we can win."

"How certain?" Buddy asked.

Lars paused before he said, "I can't guarantee it. Saying that I could would be tempting the fates. Stupidly."

Buddy dropped his voice to the low, silky part of his register. "Sure enough to bet your own soul?"

"Yes," Lars said immediately.

Yup. Boy was an idiot.

"Okay, then," Buddy said with a huge grin. "I'll have my people draw up the papers. Oh, don't look so worried. The contract's pretty simple. I'll supply you with armies. You win the war. Put the demons back on the top of the food chain where we belong. Or I claim your soul for all eternity. The end."

"Thank you," Lars said.

Boy even sounded sincere. Probably didn't even realize just how badly he'd screwed the pooch.

Expectation filled the space between them.

Buddy didn't have the patience to wait until Lars finally found the balls to say whatever else he was going to say. "Well? Out with it," Buddy said.

"Don't you want a crystal, sir?" Lars asked. "It will help your powers tremen—"

Buddy rose from his throne, then kept growing. Instead of the easy-going, potbellied demon with the funny nose, he transformed into a true Prince of Hell. His head brushed the ceiling. Great black wings expanded from his shoulders, sucking in all the light of the room. Hellfire dripped from his fingertips, scorching the floor.

A rumbling growl filled the entire throne room. Lava erupted from the walls and spewed ash and smoke into the air.

"Do not tell me, boy, that my powers need increasing,"

Beelzebub thundered. "Do not presume such familiarity with a true prince of Hell. Do you hear me?"

"Yes, yes sir, I do," Lars said.

At least the boy was smart enough to fake being scared. Buddy doubted that Lars was smart enough to realize just how close he'd come to death.

"Now, be gone," Beelzebub said. "My people will be in contact."

Lars turned and scurried out of the room as fast as his little bony feet could take him.

Beelzebub let out another belch, shooting smoke and fire toward the ceiling before he let himself shrink back down into Buddy. The throne room became a more comfortable place. Buddy's throne reappeared out of the haze and smoke.

Using on long nail, Buddy started picking at his teeth. Now, he would never go so far as to actively undermine another demon's plans to win the Great War once and for all.

That didn't mean that Buddy wouldn't poke at Lars sometimes. Remind him of his bargain.

Keep the fear of the devil in him.

CHAPTER SIX

Lars floated a few feet off the floor of his room. He was back in his human form, wearing a comfortable long-sleeved white shirt and gray slacks, with black leather boots. He had no need for a three-piece power suit and tie. Anyone who didn't understand that Lars was powerful, who underestimated him, deserved what they got.

He sat cross-legged, floating like some damned diva, just a foot above the bed.

However, never touching the ground was the best way for Lars to hide while he was here on the human plane. The Host would know immediately if Lars set foot on the human plane in his demon form. He wasn't taking a chance that they might have some ability to find him while he was in human form, either. Hence, the floating around.

Of course, the Host was looking for him. Probably had a full-scale demon hunt going on. Lars had escaped from prison, after all. One of the few who'd ever accomplished that.

The room had been set up for him by his parents. Lars was going to have to change everything. It was appropriate for the boy he'd been five years ago. (All right, if he was perfectly honest, it hadn't been totally appropriate then, either.)

However, as the general of the myriad demon armies about to fling themselves into the last Great War, it was wholly inadequate.

Lars didn't need a bed as much as a desk. He could go sleep on another plane. He needed a place where he could meet people. Talk strategy. Plan battles and discuss tactics.

Find the weak belly of the enemy and run a sharp dagger into it.

While it was more dangerous personally for Lars to be on the human plane, it was decidedly safer at the same time. Particularly since Lars' cousin Manny had discovered how to find those little pockets of space and apply corruption spells to them.

So Lars would just have to make do with this room.

The bed would just have to go. Along with the cream colored walls and the decidedly Ikea-esque end tables. The rugs, too. Not all the demons who'd be calling on him were necessarily trained not to make a mess.

They were demons. It was their job to leave messes behind everywhere they went.

One wall needed to be kept clear as a portal space.

Maps needed to be hung on the other walls, along with a trophy head or two.

Maybe Lars would leave a single spot open on the

wall, just behind his desk, to encourage his generals to do his bidding. So that he could threaten that they'd soon find their own heads in that place of honor.

Though whoever was disgracing the spot would just have to give up their place once Lars went after that damned princess troll.

In his mind's eye, *her* head took front and center stage on his wall. It was her downfall he sought, more than the human races in general, if he was perfectly honest with himself.

Something he tried not to do very often.

But since an honest mood had struck him, Lars stayed with it for a few more moments. He pulled out a pile of the gems holding the corrupt corruption spells, peering at the tiny pile of joyous maliciousness. The crystals were perfect, bright with their own glow. It wasn't until you looked deep into the heart of them that you saw the worm in the heart of the rose.

Lars sighed and put the crystals away again. He knew, *knew* that they could win with these. Given enough time and patience, the demons would not only win the Great War, but ensure their place for all eternity.

Demons generally didn't hold much weight with introspection. However, Lars hadn't had much choice. It was either go deep inside himself or go crazy while he was in solitary confinement in prison.

Or maybe he'd gone a bit of both.

So Lars had thought, and contemplated, and banged against the walls of his own head while he'd been imprisoned. He'd been allowed regular communication with his family, and it had actually been his younger brother Karl who'd perfected the corrupted corruption spell, as well as the easy twist it took to place it in a tiny crystal. (Not without Lars' help, though. Karl was not allowed to take all the credit, as much as he might occasionally brag.)

While Beelzebub and the other demons might not believe in Lars, his family *did*.

Trolls and humans weren't the only ones with Destinies, after all. Sure, Lars suspected that his father had bought the one that Lars wore, but still.

Destiny was Destiny. And it was Lars' Destiny to lead the demonic armies into the Great War.

Of course, the stupid oracles were gun-shy when it came about to predicting who would be victorious after those battles.

It didn't matter.

Lars was sure to win. He had the will. He'd taken the time to plan the attacks. The special crystals would actually guarantee their victory.

Lars' biggest problem?

Other demons.

Beelzebub's reaction to using one of the crystals had been the worst so far. Lars knew, though, that he was up for similar fights from every demon he tried to persuade.

It was like they *wanted* to lose.

None of them seemed to grasp that winning was just within reach.

While Lars had minions he could order to do his bidding slavishly, he still needed to convince the other generals and armies that it was worthwhile. No amount of demonstrations would work, either. Lars had already gone that route and failed just as spectacularly as he had earlier that week with Beelzebub. Demons were just damned stubborn.

It was bad enough trying to get a group of demons to follow a plan. Lars had heard the human expression about herding cats. He'd also heard someone upgrade the complaint to herding goldfish, which was much worse, as the damned fish moved in three dimensions.

While demons…demons were like trying to herd goldfish with fangs. Lars always had to be prepared for the ones who would jump out of the pond and bite him. Or even try to decapitate him.

All Lars could do would be to plan everything as well as possible. Plans within plans, wheels within wheels. Set it all up so that the demons *would* win the Great War.

Despite themselves.

CHAPTER SEVEN

THE GREAT KING OF THE TROLLS, KING GARETHEN, sat on his onyx throne and listened to the reports of the spring crops. Most of the court had gathered in the throne room, mainly to gossip but also to see and be seen.

It made the king's heart glad when he looked out over the trolls gathered before him. They'd slowly shaken off the influence of the corrupt chamberlain, McDommokin. The court wore bright jewel tones again—emerald greens, sapphire blues, and ruby reds—instead of the metallics that he'd favored.

The room reflected the court, with gems and precious stones, many about the size of a trollish fist, covering the ceiling and providing light. The walls were carved out of good solid rock, with a smooth floor made out of glazed rocks. The room itself was longer than it was wide, and comfortably held over two dozen trolls.

King Garethen himself had also changed styles. Gone were the blacks, browns, and somber clothing. Instead, he wore a fiery red sleeveless vest made out of the finest velvet, with crushed brown velvet pants that ended just below his knees. At least half a dozen large gold rings covered his fingers.

Under his heavy gold crown, long white hair hung down to his shoulders. His skin had a healthy green tint to it, finally, as he ate better foods again, and not the overly-refined crap that Chamberlain McDommokin had insisted on. Of course, the battle scars that ran down his arms would never heal, but healthy muscles now rose up across his shoulders, his arms, and his legs.

Before the king stood the head of the blacksmiths' guild. That guild had continued wearing black, but then again, that was their traditional color and reflected their work. The blacksmith was giving his report, as well as the guild's request for additional hard coal for the king's own forges.

King Garethen wasn't inclined to grant their request. Why had the guard put in such a large order for new weapons? The old swords worked just fine. The guard merely needed to polish them up. A bit of elbow grease and those old swords would be as good as new.

Still, at the end of the report, the king promised to "think it over" and get back to them.

The ranchers' guild was up next. They'd finally had a mild enough winter that most of the herds had survived. The number of lambs birthed that spring had gone up as well, and they actually had pigs already fat enough for slaughter, despite it only being the start of summer.

Of course, the ranchers weren't optimistic about the coming year. They were farmers (though they declared themselves as *ranchers* and therefore different) and farmers were *never* optimistic.

Though the court hearings took most of the morning once a week, King Garethen never considered it time wasted. He needed to be accessible to his subjects if he wanted to be supported by them.

Instead of appearing, as Princess Kizalynn had called him, like a sullen old man, hiding and afraid.

One of the changes King Garethen had initiated had been to listen to the complaints of common people. Not everyone, of course; that would take up all his time and he'd never get anything else done. Ever.

Instead, he'd started a lottery. That way, every citizen had a chance to appear before the king and have their grievances heard.

To ensure that the lottery would be run fairly as well, he'd put the king's guard in charge of it and *not* any member of the court. There would have been too much temptation for a member of the court to start taking bribes, while the king's guard took great pride in being incorruptible.

However, for the most part, the common troll had no idea how to speak in court, let alone address the king. An unfortunate consequence was that some in the court came just for those moments of inadvertent hilarity.

Today's complaint came courtesy of a troll called Lapundar, who was a candlemaker. He was short for a troll, and thin. Almost as if he was part human, a suggestion that the king would *never* make to the troll's face.

Not unless he wanted to be subject to another duel and kill yet another of his subjects.

But Lapundar was obviously making good money at what he did. He wore a beautiful sleeveless tunic made of a rich blue, green, and gold paisley. His pants were black velvet. He didn't wear any rings on his fingers, however, he did have two gold hoops piercing his right ear.

"My sovereign liege," Lapundar said, bowing after he was introduced by the crier. "I bring you gifts only fit for someone as elevated as yourself."

Lapundar nodded to a young boy, maybe seven years old, and shy. The boy slowly walked forward, carrying a beautiful hand-carved box, about a foot square.

"What a strapping lad you have there!" the king exclaimed.

"Eh," Lapundar said. "He's the best I can afford."

"I see," the king said. He was surprised. Normally, merchants apprenticed their own family and rarely took on strangers. Particularly not hired help.

The boy looked around anxiously, as if unsure what to do next.

"Open the box," Lapundar declared. "Show the king our finest work."

The boy lifted the hinged lid and showed the king, then turned in a circle so the rest of the court could see as well.

Four tall, off-white candles lay snuggled against rich red velvet. Many small gems were embedded in the wax, along with crystals that shown with their own light.

"A candle for every season, my liege," Lapundar said.

King Garethen could see that now. Green spring, blue

summer, orange fall, and blue-white winter. Each seasonal candle had its own pattern of designs, like ferns, waterfalls, leaves, and snowflakes.

The gems seemed to wink at King Garethen. No, that had to be his imagination or a trick of the light. The candles had no magic. Trolls, particularly commoners, for the most part weren't magical.

"A kingly gift, indeed," King Garethen said, nodding. "Thank you. Place this in the hall of viewing, so that everyone can see your magnificent work."

"Thank you, my liege, thank you," Lapundar said, bowing his head low.

The king actually received a lot of gifts. The hall of viewing was reserved for the best of those. Merchants whose goods were placed there would certainly not stay quiet about it.

Most of the gifts the king received were immediately regifted to others in the court, the king's relatives, or to cement relations with other *kith and kin* kingdoms.

These candles, though, the king might actually keep.

"What need have you to seek your king today?" King Garethen asked as one of his own stewards took away the box with the candles.

"As you would expect from any honest businessman, I have a concern with our taxes, my liege," Lapundar said. He immediately launched into a lengthy complaint about how the costs of everything kept rising and he couldn't just keep charging his customers more and more for the same basic goods, now could he?

"But what would you have me do?" the king asked. "We need roads. And the children need to be taught. And you certainly wouldn't want me to leave our borders undefended, now would you?"

"That's the problem," Lapundar said. "Demons haven't threatened our borders for years. The worlds are at peace. The demons have been stopped."

"For now," the king agreed. "They will come back."

"When they do, we'll all gladly contribute to the war coffers!" Lapundar said. "But until then? How large of a standing army do we actually need?"

"Thank you for your opinion, citizen," King Garethen said, dismissing the man. "You've given me food for thought."

After the court had been dismissed, King Garethen sat on his throne in the empty hall for a while. He was used to sitting there with no hope. Before Christine had come back into his life, or rather, Princess Kizalynn.

She'd taught him many things, this new daughter of his. He'd declared her his official heir, going through the intricate ritual that spring. The other cousins, for the most part, took it well. Particularly Timolok, who *had* been next in line. He, too, was a farmer, and it was nearly impossible to bring him into court except during the winter. And even then, he'd complain about the work he was leaving undone.

King Garethen still didn't talk with his brother Te'Dur, Kizalynn's biological father. That traitor now lived with the gatekeeper, Rodericket, who maintained the gate on this side of the fairy troll bridge.

Rodericket was at least someone the king could trust and made regular reports on Te'Dur to the king's guard, which got forwarded right away to the king.

While some of the court had been against the king's choice of heir, most of their objections had been, quite frankly, politically motivated. It wasn't because they considered her a bad choice. However, they'd married into the royal family with hopes of being closer to the throne. Once Kizalynn had been declared the king's heir, their positions had diminished, as her family would be in line for the throne now.

The king knew that Lapundar was wrong. They needed those border guards.

However, did the kingdom need as many guards as they had? Ozlandia, the head of the king's guard, would say that they did.

On the one hand, it had been five years since Lars and the other demons had been stopped and the Great War averted.

On the other hand, they were demons. They would come back. Even if it took one hundred years. They'd return for yet another fight.

King Garethen reached up and ran his fingertips against the rough edge of the broken tusk sticking up from his bottom jaw.

He remembered the battles. His brother Te'Dur, traitor though he may be, still bore the scars of Hell fire. Demons had set Kizalynn's crib on fire, and Te'Dur had risked his own life to save his daughter. Then had made the difficult choice to allow her to become a changeling, the only way Te'Dur could see to save his daughter's life.

Kizalynn bore similar scars on her arms.

The demons would be back.

How much did the king need to prepare before they returned? And at what cost?

———

KING GARETHEN MET WITH OZLANDIA AND Alberthendi, the head of the king's guard and her second in command, in his private study just after lunch. The walls held cases for scrolls and beautiful stones. Thin slits for windows on one wall looked out over the back gardens of the palace. A large geode—about three feet in diameter—hung from the wall directly behind the king. He liked all that solid rock behind him. It was a pretty purple color, with clear crystals in the center of it.

The desk had been shaped out of solid stone, a great boulder of granite perfectly carved to fit the height of the king. The top had been polished so diligently that it reflected the flame of the oil lamp sitting on the corner of it. Scents of spicy lamb and turnip stew floated across the air now and again, leftovers from a very fine lunch.

The king didn't have papers strewn across his desk. He wasn't a merchant. Instead, he had a small notebook that he used for jotting down a few notes now and again, just to jog his memory when he needed to.

His memory was much better than a human's. However, that didn't mean he always remembered everything.

A solid, comfortable chair sat behind the desk, and two more on the other side. They were all made from iron and leather—mere wood would have groaned and protested and eventually given up the ghost after having to support the weight of trolls day in and day out.

Ozlandia came in first, wearing the outfit of a standard guard, with a navy-blue jacket and breeches, thick black boots, and a peaked metal helmet. She had her long, double-headed ax tied to her back. In addition, net bags full of sharp rocks hung from her belt, as a troll could accurately hit just about anything they aimed for.

She was tall for a commoner, as most of the truly tall trolls came from royalty. She wore her brown hair short and straight, barely long enough for anyone to grab during a fight. Her two lower tusks were scratched but not broken. Her brown eyes glowed with an internal fierceness that the king had come to respect.

Alberthendi came in second. He frequently traveled through all of Trollville, so was dressed more like a commoner in a plain, off-white muslin shirt and brown wool pants. However, he also bore a long, wickedly curved sword on his left side and the bag of stones on his right.

"My king," Alberthendi said, bowing low as he came into the room.

"Sit, sit," King Garethen directed from his side of the desk. "So what reports do you have for me?"

The two guards exchanged a worried glance.

"I'm not going to like this, am I?" the king said with a sigh.

"No, but it's an easy enough request to deny," Ozlandia said. "We've been approached by the cambions to the west of the kingdom."

King Garethen sighed. The cambions were creatures

that were half demon, half human. They were unpleasant to look at, as they appeared as really ugly humans. However, they weren't as bad as some of the other demon races. He wouldn't trust a large group of them, but individually, they were frequently not that bad. No worse than humans.

"What do they want?" the king asked.

"They want direct access to the fairy troll bridge," Ozlandia said.

"Why on dear solid ground would they want that?" the king asked. "They aren't any more welcome on the human plane as anywhere else."

Alberthendi shrugged. "Don't know. Not sure what their scheme is."

"Is there a scheme? Some dark plot?" King Garethen asked.

"There must be," Ozlandia said firmly. "Otherwise, why would they ask?"

"Just for the convenience?" the king proposed.

"No, I'm sure there's something else going on," Alberthendi said.

"There always is," the king replied.

The two guards stared at him.

"There's always a dark plot out there. Something to end the world as we know it. However, we haven't had a good battle in years." The king narrowed his eyes and stared hard, first at Alberthendi then at Ozlandia. "I had a complaint from a merchant today about taxes."

They both gave him perplexed looks.

"I know, I know. If there's one thing that all merchants have in common, it's complaints about taxes," the king continued. "The complaints are as constant as the morning sunlight, coming every day, it seems."

King Garethen sighed. "I have not forgotten that it is demons we're fighting. Demons who would like to tear everything apart and remake the world as their own personal garbage pile. But how prepared do we need to be? Is constant vigilance the answer? Particularly when the threat remains nebulous?"

He had their attention now.

"I know you requested hard coal for making more swords," the king continued. "Again, why do you need to be so heavily armed? What is the point?"

King Garethen looked from one guard to the other. Neither replied. "Someone? Anyone?"

"Sire, the threat is real," Ozlandia said slowly. "We need to be prepared."

"Does it make sense to make all those swords now? Or just make them as we need them?" the king countered. "As the merchant said this morning, they'll all gladly contribute to the war coffers once war starts. In the meanwhile? They think it's all going into useless weapons and feeding soldiers we don't need."

"Demons are trained as fighters from a young age," Alberthendi pointed out. "Trolls are tough. I'd take an untrained army of trolls against a crowd of demons any day. However, taking a group of *trained* trolls is an even better advantage."

The king nodded. He could see Alberthendi's point. He understood that it was better to be more prepared than less.

He still wasn't sure what level of prepared they needed to be at.

"How many trolls guard our borders?" the king asked. "And what would happen if we halved that number?"

Ozlandia looked shocked. Alberthendi just looked stubborn.

"Go work the numbers," the king directed them. "Figure out the scenarios. Does it make sense to keep so many trolls employed there? How many are actually doing patrols? Or tending to their crops and their cattle instead?"

"Sire, we just had a few who weren't actually patrolling," Ozlandia protested.

It hadn't been that long ago when some of the border patrol had been reported on by their neighbors for no longer doing their jobs, but instead pocketing the gold paid to them and only focusing on their own crops instead.

"And by now, how many more have slipped into bad habits?" the king asked. "I think it's better to keep a smaller team who are more sharply trained. So it will be easier to monitor them. When there's a real, obvious threat, of course, we will recruit more trolls."

"But we can't patrol everywhere!" Ozlandia complained.

"You can't patrol everywhere now," King Garethen pointed out. "You patrol each area, what, once every two weeks or so?"

"Then we need more trolls, not less," Alberthendi said.

"No," King Garethen said firmly. "Just get me the numbers. Let's do some serious planning. And see what the minimum number is that you actually need."

He dismissed the guards, then pulled his notebook over to him. He recorded the date along with a note about not merely halving the border patrol, but also halving the army.

That would save him quite a few gold coins. He would have a very large war chest when the time came.

Before that time came (and he knew without doubt that it would) he had better uses for such coins.

CHAPTER EIGHT

Christine fumed as she cast around for a new portal site to transport herself to.

Redmond was getting so built up! It used to be easy to find an alley or the back of a small shop to transport herself into, even as little as six months ago. Now, there was construction everywhere. Huge new buildings that didn't take to magic well.

Finally, Christine found that the backdoor to Victor's coffeeshop was still available. It wasn't like the International District, where the demons had been closing every portal off. No, it was actually the humans destroying the old portal sites, and no one taking the time to build new ones.

Progress, they called it.

Bah.

Christine stood before the gateway in the Japanese Garden in the Arboretum. Twisted vines had been trained up the sides of a *tori* gate. To the right stood the path through the northern part of the garden, and just past that was the pond. To the left a grove of bamboo made soft clicking noises as the wind blew through.

The gate itself had a slight shimmer to it, as though it had been slicked with rain. Fortunately, it had actually stopped raining that afternoon, though it hadn't gotten warm. Maybe the weather would become more June-like later, but Christine wasn't hopeful.

Every other state in the United States has been experiencing warmer than normal weather.

Not Washington, however. No, they continued to be colder than normal.

Fortunately, Christine didn't feel the cold so much. Particularly in her troll form. Even the rain didn't bother her as much as it once had, not when her water element deep inside her rejoiced at it.

Still, Christine wore a cute, bright purple raincoat that hung down to her knees, along with her typical human jeans. Underneath the coat, she had on a bright mint-green turtleneck that showed off her curves.

It had taken her a few years to accept just how *zoftig* she appeared. Despite the fact that she could have taken any form, her inner troll liked this form the best. Christine just had to accept that she was not human, and that their standards of beauty did not apply to her. It made her look different than Tina as well, and that was a good thing, though usually people did assume they were sisters.

Keeping her destination now firmly in mind, Christine stepped through the gate and into Redmond. It was actually raining here. Christine pulled her hood up to cover her head, then headed down the busy street to the restaurant where she was meeting Tina for dinner.

Every Thursday was "girls' night out." They tried a new-to-them restaurant, sticking primarily to Seattle at first, then expanding into the suburbs. They'd made some spectacular finds, as well as some restaurants that they couldn't even be paid to return to.

Christine was aware that at some level, she was still rebelling against the changeling spell that had forced her to always be the same, to be afraid of going anywhere new, trying anything different.

Tina felt guilty about how Christine had been used, adopted by the Zimmermans then transformed into a changeling, and so bravely stood at Christine's side trying everything new as well, despite the fact that she was also shy about doing different things.

(Although Christine *had* been the only one of the pair of them to get her hair permed. And now Tina understood what a bad idea it was for either of them.)

Tina was already waiting at the restaurant when Christine arrived. It was a cute place, with fake license plates hanging on the walls, listing the various dishes. Large booths made out of solid wood filled the center of the restaurant. Colorful flags—they looked like Tibetan prayer flags—hung over the booths.

"Hi!" Christine said as she slid into the booth opposite Tina.

Tina looked much better than she had when she'd first "lost" her Destiny. Her pale cheeks held regular color now, and her blue eyes frequently had their old sparkle.

Though not today.

Christine sighed silently and kept her own smile bright as she asked Tina, "How are you?"

She knew something was wrong, and that sooner or later, she'd get a serious earful.

Then again, that was what friends were for. For Tina to have a bad day and complain, or for Christine to do the same. They also shared their joys, like how much Tina loved Nicky, as well as how Christine enjoyed all her martial training.

"I'm okay," Tina admitted, rocking her head from side to side. She wore a cute, lowcut pale red shirt that emphasized just how pale Tina had gotten lately (something Christine wasn't convinced was healthy) along with a pretty gold chain with a tiny heart in the center, a present from Nicky.

Christine felt a little bit of relief at Tina's reaction. If Tina was in a really bad place, she'd either admit it right away, or more likely, would completely deny it until Christine teased it out of her.

"How are you?" Tina asked, glancing up from the menu and smiling at her friend.

"I'm good," Christine said. She was worried about her dad—less worried than Dennis, as she hadn't really seen anything wrong with Dad. And she hadn't heard anything troubling in the news of all the planes.

Her news primarily came from talking with all the travelers who came through the gate. Really, if someone would just listen to her and create a newsletter that just had current events going on in most of the major worlds, they'd make a lot of money from the ex-pats who no longer lived in their particular plane.

If Christine was being honest, though, most of the ex-pats would never read such a newsletter, let alone pay for it. The humans were the ones who wrote everything down. Christine had frequently bemoaned the fact that most of the other races didn't even have *books* for her to read and learn about them.

As a former librarian, she remained morally offended by the other races' lack of the written word. Even if she'd had to spend money to translate any works that she did find.

She considered it one of her greatest personal failings. Despite how much Christine loved books and reading, she wasn't very good at languages. She'd finally had to admit defeat after learning just a few words in Orcish, Elvish, as well as the most common of the demons' tongues (because of course each demon race had to have its own language to prove themselves special.)

"Gosh, everything looks good here!" Tina said as she perused the menu some more.

They finally agreed on splitting a fried plantain appetizer, while Christine got the pulled pork and Tina got the soup of the day.

"So how is your training going?" Tina asked.

Christine could tell that Tina was being deliberately cheerful.

Still, Christine replied, "Good!" She knew that Tina would build up to her complaint, so Christine launched into a description of her latest accomplishment, which had included not only a spinning jump with a swiping blow but landing without falling over.

After they ordered, Tina told Christine of her latest fight with Nicky about the Pride Parade that weekend. "She just doesn't understand how I have no desire whatsoever to go and hang out in huge crowds! It isn't that I'm not proud, or something."

Christine nodded in sympathy. That was actually one of the ways in which they were similar. Neither of them found being in large, loud, crowded spaces all that fun. Instead, they liked quieter events with fewer people.

While Christine had pushed herself to go out more frequently, out to clubs or more disastrously that one dance class she'd taken, it hadn't been the changeling spell that had enforced that effect. She was just naturally introverted, as was Tina.

Something they both had to overcome in their respective roles.

They paused for a short time while the food was served. It was absolutely delicious, the plantains nicely crispy with a good spicy dipping sauce, Christine's pork well-seasoned. Even the rice was delicious, much better than Christine had had at the overly Americanized Chinese restaurant they'd gone to the week before.

Since changing into a troll, Christine's taste buds had gone through a major shift. All bread now tasted like cardboard. Pasta had no flavor whatsoever. Even pizza wasn't any good. Instead, Christine had shifted her diet into more meat and vegetables. She joked sometimes that what she ate now could be described as, "Dead critter. Fresh veggies."

"So how is your magic training going?" Christine asked after a bit, as she always did. Being able to perform magic was so important to Tina. It was like Christine's ability with ax and stone, so much a part of her that she couldn't imagine ever doing without it again.

Tina sighed.

Uh oh.

A few weeks before, Tina had complained about how wonky her magic had been that day. Was she still having problems?

Christine foresaw a really dark future for the pair of them if Tina lost her magical ability.

Quite frankly, Christine wasn't convinced that Tina would still have the will to live if she could no longer perform magic.

"The thing is, I'd had that big fight with Nicky, right?" Tina said all in a rush. "So I was looking for some comfort. Now, normally I'd be able to scry in just about anybody. I tried to look in on one of my old mentors. Malcom. I've told you about him, right?"

Christine nodded. She'd actually met Malcom at one of their shared birthday parties. He'd been a lovely older gentleman who treated everyone with dignity. She couldn't think of another way to describe him.

She could totally understand why Tina had felt the need to look in on Malcom, how that might bring her some peace. Malcom was like that.

Hell, if Christine really needed that sort of calm, she might go and visit Malcom. And be welcomed, she was certain, even though she wasn't a human magic user.

"But my spell fizzled when I tried it." Tina shook her head. "I still don't know why. Maybe he's gotten himself some stronger protection. It didn't feel that way, though. The spell didn't bounce off something hard. Instead, it felt like I was trying to shoot a tiny stream of flame through a waterfall."

"Okay," Christine said. That struck her as odd. Tina was the strongest magician she knew. That most people knew. What was going on?

"So I needed to check and see if it was my magic that was being wonky or if it was Malcom. I tried the scry spell again on someone else."

Christine heard the guilt in Tina's voice. "Who?" Christine asked, her curiosity warring with her sense of dread.

"Your dad. Our dad," Tina said, a touch of defensiveness creeping into her voice.

"Okay," Christine said. "Did you get through?"

"I did," Tina admitted. "But this is where it gets weird."

Though Tina shouldn't have done it, because it was such a violation of her parents' privacy, Christine was kind of glad that Tina had tried. It meant that Christine needed to improve the spells protecting her parents. Strengthen them. While there weren't going to be many demons who were stronger than Tina, if she could get through, others might as well.

"What do you mean by weird?" Christine said, bracing herself.

"So your—I mean, Dad was there in the living room, working on one of his models. This was Monday," she added.

Christine nodded, slightly concerned that Tina hadn't called her with the news of something weird with her/their dad.

"And it was like he could *see* me. He walked right over

to the spot I was scrying through and put his thumb up over it, like he was squashing a bug," Tina said.

"Maybe your scrying spell had a reaction with one of the protection spells that I already have set up in the room," Christine speculated. "So maybe it was visible or something." It didn't seem likely, but it might have been possible. She'd have to check with Nik to see what he thought.

Tina looked surprised. "I hadn't considered that!" She paused, then shook her head. "No, that wasn't the weirdest part." She seemed to be bracing herself as well. "When he touched the spot, the spell collapsed. It shouldn't have done that. Not at all. The spell should have remained intact."

"What does that mean?" Christine asked slowly, a sense of dread crawling up between her shoulder blades, making her palms itch for her ax.

"It means Dad might have magic," Tina finally replied.

"Magic?" Christine said. Okay, possibly shouted.

"Shhhh," Tina said, lowering her head as if to hide herself. "Yes. Magic."

"Swell," was all that Christine could think to say. "How do we check?"

"I think we should arrange for him to meet Malcom for coffee or tea or something. Malcom would know," Tina said.

"How about I just take him to see Nik?" Christine offered. "Shouldn't he be able to detect it as well?"

Tina shrugged. "I don't know. Nik isn't human, after all. If the magic is really faint, he might not be able to catch a trace of it. Only a human magician would be able to do that."

"Okay," Christine said easily, though she was planning on taking her dad to see Nik as well.

Nik had reiterated more than once that Christine could never trust a human. After Tina had turned on Christine and started trying to kill her because of demonic influence, Christine had come to understand exactly what Nik had meant.

"Do you think that Dad has always had some sort of magical abilities? Or was it latent until now? Only expressing itself because he's been exposed to so much magic these last five years?" Christine asked.

Tina shrugged. "That's something we can ask Malcom about."

"Maybe Dad would have come into his magic earlier if we hadn't been switched at birth," Christine said without thinking about it. "Didn't Mrs. Zimmerman once complain about how you would even glow in your crib?"

Tina's smile was brittle. "Maybe."

Christine reached over across the table and squeezed Tina's hand, despite the fact that neither of them much cared for being touched.

"I didn't mean it like that," Christine insisted. "Don't take it like you messed up his life by not being there. You were a baby. It wasn't your fault."

Tina nodded and said, "I know."

Christine just managed to avoid not rolling her eyes. Tina was obviously lying. The possibility that she'd messed up Dad's life by not being there, despite the fact that she had been just a baby and that the Zimmermans had been the ones to cook up the scheme, would drive Tina into a fast downward spiral.

"You be sure you tell your therapist," Christine insisted. She squeezed Tina's hand one more time before releasing it.

Though Christine would stand by Tina through thick and thin, there really wasn't much she could do about some of Tina's issues.

Nik's words came again, ringing through Christine's head. Though she knew that Nik was wrong, she had to acknowledge that in this, he was also right.

Never trust a human.

CHAPTER NINE

Vern Tuckerman wouldn't admit it to anyone, not his daughter, his son, or even his wife. He could barely admit it to himself.

But Vern no longer felt, well, *swell* all the time.

It had been part of the reason why he'd taken a partial retirement from the insurance agency. He found he had a lot of difficulty concentrating on the paperwork, on clients, gosh, on anything. He kept getting distracted by absolutely nothing, like the other day when he could have sworn there was a spider on the wall, even though there wasn't, not even after he'd squashed it. Even his beloved RC planes were getting more and more difficult to put together.

After he assembled the wings, the next step had been to glue on a strong, bright red, plastic. Then he would use a steamer to shrink the plastic tighter between the struts.

For the craziest time, Vern had thought about not using the steamer, but just running his hand over the plastic to see if he could get better results. As if he could somehow superheat his palms or something.

Crazy talk, right?

Vern didn't think he was just getting old and forgetful, though he suspected that his son Dennis believed that. Lizzie, his wife, also sometimes gave him strange looks. Well, stranger looks than usual. You'd think that after enjoying holy matrimony with him for almost forty years that she would have gotten used to him by then.

That afternoon, Vern sat in the living room on the sofa, looking out over the lake. Which was another difference. Since when had he gotten to be the guy who stared off into space, communing with nature?

He'd kind of been switching over his wardrobe as well. Gone were the nice long-sleeved shirts that he wore into the office. He found himself favoring, well, T-shirts. That just wasn't cool. He was the kind of guy who was into short-sleeved Polo shirts. The jeans were the same. And barefoot was everybody's thing, right?

Vern knew that he should be getting up, off the couch. Both Christine and Tina were coming over later that afternoon, taking him out for happy hour at Mike's Pub, just down the street. They did that from time to time, just hanging out with ol' Dad.

But Vern found his butt planted firmly in the couch, attached there with straps. He wasn't exhausted. Not really. Just...something inside him felt tired all the time. Like he was fighting something off. He wasn't sick, at least not as far as he could tell.

He sniffed experimentally, only smelling the baloney, garlic mayonnaise, and cheese sandwich that he'd had for lunch, along with a handful of carrots and two sour dill pickles. But he wasn't congested. He went jogging most every morning and still managed three miles every day, even though he had to be much more careful about not actually running into the lake now than ever before.

Without telling anyone, Vern had made an appointment with his doctor the next week to get some blood tests done.

Better to find out the worst now rather than later, particularly if it was the big C word.

Though no one in his family had ever had cancer, at least as far as he was aware. His own father had owned a car dealership and been a complete alcoholic, dying young from cirrhosis of the liver. His mother had passed over a decade before, unhappy to the very end.

It was part of why Vern made his own language, his own fun. Why he refused to care what other people thought of him. Both his parents had been far too concerned with what the neighbors thought, and had spent money on things for keeping up with the Joneses instead of on what would bring them joy.

Vern, if he was truly being honest with himself, didn't give a fuck about the Joneses, or anyone outside of the family, for that matter.

Something else he had never bothered saying out loud to anyone, not even Lizzie.

The door opened before Vern could completely lose his head in his own meditations.

"Hey, pumpkin!" Vern said, surging off the couch and coming over to greet his daughter.

No, both of his daughters. He considered Tina as

much a part of the family as Christine, even though she'd been raised by other humans.

"How are you?" Vern asked, first giving his troll daughter a quick hug, then his human daughter.

And that was one of the weirdest things of all. Vern had always been a touchy-feely guy. He loved holding hands with Lizzie when they walked. Yet, he now no longer wanted to even shake hands with his co-workers.

"Good, good," Tina said. She seemed shy this afternoon. Well, more shy than usual.

"So let's go!" Vern said after he slipped on his coat. The sky was only overcast at the moment, but they'd surely get more rain before evening.

"You're ready?" Christine asked, giving him a strange look.

"Ready as ever!" Vern replied happily.

"Aren't you forgetting something?" Christine said, looking down pointedly at Vern's feet.

"Oh. Oh! Gosh darn it!" Vern said. He gave a shrug. "I've just been feeling so carefree these days! Not having to work all the time," he added with a wink as he slipped his loafers on. "Do I pass inspection?" Vern asked. He spread his arms wide and invited them to look closely at him. "Am I groovy enough to hang out with you two cats?"

Christine rolled her eyes at him. "You know that no one ever used that language except in movies, right?"

"Whateves," Vern said, deliberately using the modern vernacular.

"It won't just be us, this afternoon," Christine warned as they walked out the door. "We're meeting one of Tina's old mentors for drinks as well."

"Is everything okay?" Vern asked. He wished that Tina hadn't just turned her back to go down the stairs. He wanted to be able to read her expression.

And where had that come from? It wasn't that he couldn't read faces. But it had never been as important to him before.

"Malcom is getting older," Tina explained. "And he's really important to me. So I want to make sure that you get to meet him."

"But I did meet him already," Vern said. "Tall black gentleman? It was at your shared Brightday party. Two, no, three years ago."

"That's right," Christine said. "You did meet him at our birthday party."

"No," Vern said, shaking his head. "It was a Brightday party. Where you celebrate the light captured inside each of you."

Christine and Tina exchanged a glance, but Vern knew he was right.

His daughters, both of them, shone with such an incredible light and grace, brightening up even the most cloudy of days.

He could see it almost all the time now, which was one of the changes that he was actually thankful for.

"Magic? Really? Me?" Vern said. He tried to keep his voice down. They were in a public place after all. They sat in a circular booth in the far corner of the pub. The windows nearby showed that it had, indeed, started raining in earnest. The rest of the room was half filled, surprising for a Friday night. Then again, given another hour or so and the party was likely to have started in earnest. In the meanwhile, there was one office group nosily toasting each other at the far side of the room, another couple of tables were filled with tourists, while four of the regulars sat at the bar.

"Yes, sir, you," Malcom said. His quiet, gentle voice was easy to pick out, even in the loud pub. "Now, I don't detect a great deal of magic there. But you have a spark buried deep inside of you."

"Well, gosh darn it all!" Vern said. He just couldn't believe it. "Has it always been there?"

Malcom shrugged his elegant shoulders. He wore a nice white shirt under an actual argyle knit vest, done in a diamond pattern of gold on navy blue, with green highlights. Silver tipped the black hair at his temples. His face was long and expressive, kind eyes peering out of a broad forehead, with lots of laugh wrinkles creasing his the corners of his eyes and mouth.

Vern guessed that Malcom was probably in his sixties, though he could have been eighty. Despite the wrinkles, his black skin still had a youthful appearance to it.

"We don't know if you've always had magic, Dad, and we possibly never will," Christine said. "If it's okay with you, we'll go visit Nik later, have him take a look too." Christine raised her chin stubbornly, glancing at Tina, who just rolled her eyes.

"That would be swell," Vern said. He remembered the little wooden man, and had been fascinated by the magic shop.

"So, Vern, have you been distracted lately?" Malcom asked.

Vern thought for a moment before deciding to tell the truth. "I have been," he admitted. "I was afraid it was something else. You know. Something much worse."

"It's probably just the magic awakening inside you," Malcom said.

"I don't have to go to the doctor then?" Vern said, wanting clarification. Would the doctor be able to detect the magic in Vern's blood? Probably not, not if they'd never been able to detect the troll in Christine's.

"Oh, I'd still go see your doctor," Malcom said, smiling at him. "Better to make sure that the old engine is still ticking along without an issue."

"Got it," Vern said. He took another sip of his mojito. Golly willikers! Magic! He just couldn't get over it. What was he going to tell Lizzie?

"What's the next step?" Vern asked after a moment.

"That depends on you," Tina said firmly. "You should get some basic training, though."

"She's right," Malcom added. "An untrained magician can be a danger to himself and his family."

"What kind of danger?" Vern said, alarmed.

"You won't be burning down the house anytime soon with some sort of accidental fireball," Malcom said, trying to reassure him. "You just need some focus training so you'll be better able to concentrate."

"That would be great," Vern said. Anything would be better than feeling as though he was losing his groove.

"Will he be able to check and strengthen the

protection spells around the house? Once he gets some training?" Christine asked.

Vern nodded. Though he didn't understand his daughter's apprehension about this Great War that was supposedly coming, he knew it was real enough to her. He would love to be able to take on some of her worry, to lift at least some of the stress off her shoulders.

"I don't know," Malcom said. "Are the charms human in nature?"

All the time before, when Christine or Tina had talked about the differences between human and troll magic, Vern had tried to stay politely interested.

Suddenly, he might have a vested interest in the subject.

"Mostly trollish," Christine admitted. "But there are a couple of human distraction charms thrown in as well."

"You need to take those down," Malcom said urgently. "Those will inhibit your father's ability. Particularly while he's so new to magic."

"All of the house defenses?" Christine asked.

Vern didn't like how worried she suddenly got.

"No, not all of them. The troll ones should be fine. Just the human spells," Malcom said slowly.

"It all seems so complicated," Vern said after a moment. That he had magic! And now had to have training. It might explain a lot of things, such as why he'd always felt so disconnected from his own parents. Why he'd been so diligent at forming his own use of words and language.

"It isn't," Malcom assured him. "Your magical nature will rise quickly, once you start training."

"Okay," Vern said. "So, where do I find a teacher? Do I advertise on Craigslist or something?"

Tina laughed. "No, silly. Malcom will teach you."

Vern was pleased that Malcom looked as surprised as he felt.

"I don't want to be an imposition—" Vern started to say.

"No, no, I think she's right," Malcom said after a moment. "I trained Tina when she was young, just learning magic. Though I'm officially retired," he said, pausing to give Tina what could best be called a stink eye, "I believe that training an old dog new tricks might be fun."

Vern snorted. "Better than teaching youngsters who think they know it all?"

Malcom laughed. "Exactly."

They arranged to meet the following Monday at Malcom's house. Then Malcom had to leave. He was going dancing that night with his main squeeze, Adele, who he appeared to just be dating, as he was single and had remained so his entire life.

After Malcom had left, Vern and the girls waited for Lizzie to come join them. Vern felt as though sparkling wine ran through his veins instead of plain blood.

"Did you suspect? Before?" he asked Christine while they waited.

Christine shook her head. "Dennis thought there was something wrong. I told him he was imagining things."

"Dennis worries," Vern admitted. "So do you."

"I'm afraid that you're going to be more vulnerable until you finish your training," Christine admitted.

"What?" Vern said. "I'm totally going to rock it." He gave her a huge grin, just to watch her roll her eyes at him.

The family had survived Christine "coming out" as a troll. He and Lizzie were still rock solid, maybe more so after the long heart-to-heart talks that they'd had the last few years.

The Tuckermans could survive another magician in the family.

It was going to be kind of groovy.

CHAPTER TEN

Ty Brooks, demon-hunter extraordinaire, sprinted for his life.

Who would have thought that the *Rinwrathkitum* demons in their juvenile form were so fast? Particularly since the adults looked like slow-moving limestone boulders? Complete with yellow rock full of holes that crumbled quickly?

Seemed that their youngsters, however, were more like flying granite birds, with narrow, knife-like wings and long, wickedly-sharp beaks.

Some demons just had messed up morphology.

Ty had gone hunting for his most recent bond jumper in the pocket world that the *Rinwrathkitum* had claimed as their own. The land was made up of an arpeggio of desolate rock islands surrounded by cold gray oceans. The water appeared to be part of their birth cycle as well.

Oh, and had he mentioned that the oceans were inhabited by death sharks that made the huge killer sharks on earth seem like kittens in comparison?

He hadn't laid eyes on his prey yet, though he knew that the jumper was there. He could smell the demon. He just had to find the stupid son of a bitch before the demon hopped planes again.

Ty wasn't a full lycanthrope—he hadn't originally been human, bitten by a werewolf. Instead, he'd been born to a lycanthrope and a human, so he was only one quarter werewolf. Then, his human father had insisted that Ty go through strict training, starting as a child, so that he didn't react to the moon curse and instead, could change shape when needed.

More than one werewolf considered Ty an abomination.

He had no use for old farts so tied to tradition that they'd chain their own kids to the same hopeless cycle of man-monster. Instead, he continued his training and meditation so he was always in control of the beast within. This made him not only an oddity in his clan, but in the world in general. He wasn't human, he wasn't one of the *kith and kin*, and he wasn't part of the Host or a demon.

He was always the odd being out, and he was okay with that.

Currently, Ty was in his half-changed form. His nose was pushed out into a dog's snout, as black as his skin. He could follow a lot more scents when he was like this. He'd let his ears transform as well, growing up into points on the top of his skull, able to swivel and gather more sounds. His hands had grown a little bigger and black claws now tipped his fingers. But he'd kept the rest of himself the same.

A shrieking noise from above and behind Ty made

him bend over as he kept running. One of those damned juveniles nearly strafed him, the obsidian sharp talons putting yet *another* tear into Ty's leather jacket.

Damn it! This bond was just getting too expensive.

But once Ty had the scent in his nose, he found it difficult to just give up the trail.

The ground under Ty's good boots was rough, full of small pebbles that would make him slide down a slope at exactly the wrong time. The sky was a yellowish white, with thin trails of clouds riding high. It didn't smell exactly like rotten eggs, but close.

The smell of shit from the juveniles was much stronger, with a sour, rotten-yogurt smell.

Yet, under all that was an even ranker odor. Like someone who made a habit of eating spoiled cabbage had just taken a shit. It was eye-wateringly foul.

Impressive, really.

Ty hadn't meant to disturb the "kids" on the rock face. But he'd thought that the jumper had been there. Or at least had passed by recently.

Had probably been chased off, just like Ty was.

Buggers were persistent, too, and had continued chasing Ty even after he'd covered, what, half the island already?

At least he thought the scent of the jumper was now ahead of him, instead of behind him. Or had the winds just carried the demon's scent in a weird pattern?

Ty stayed low to the ground, not climbing any of the short hills he ran by. He'd learned quickly that the birds didn't like dropping down so close to the earth.

Finally, Ty spied what looked like a trail going down

the side of one of the hills, leading to what looked like a cave at the far end.

The stench of sour cabbage wafted up toward him.

Got you now.

It didn't surprise Ty to see the demon sulking just inside the mouth of the cave.

It did surprise him when the demon waved his claws in the air and said, "Yoo hoo! I'm over here!"

Ty paused for just a moment, only to be hit solidly on the back by another one of the damned birds.

"I'm not trying to hurt you!" he yelled at the damned flock.

They didn't seem to understand that as the next one was already dive bombing toward him.

Ty knew if he started fighting the birds, more would come. And more. And more. There would be too many for him. It would be like something from one of those bad human horror films.

Never mind that Ty and his kind were frequently monsters as well in those same flicks.

Instead, Ty turned and ran again, slaloming down the trail toward the opening of the cave. More than one bird brushed by the side of his shoulder, unable to get a claw in.

"This way!" the demon shouted.

Ty didn't have any choice. He turned at the last minute and swerved right into the cave, running full tilt, trusting that he'd be able to stop quickly enough.

Before the demon could ambush him, at any rate.

Ty still ran into a rock wall, bouncing back hard. At least he landed on his feet. Man, that was gonna leave some nasty bruises. He turned around quickly, claws out, ready to take on all newcomers.

However, the demon in question didn't seem to be intent on killing Ty. Not at all.

Instead, the demon rushed over to where Ty was now standing. "Are you all right? Are you hurt?" He genuinely looked concerned, which was kind of a funny expression on a face with a single eye bulging from the center of his forehead and a mouth full of nasty teeth. The demon wore ragged breeches, looking like a reject from the Renaissance Festival. He had welts and boils running down both arms and his chest, constantly bleeding pus.

Yup. That was the source of the demon's stench.

Ty rolled one shoulder, then the other. "Nothing that a good long soak in Epson salts won't cure," he said. He tugged at his jacket and tried to see the slashes across the back of it. "This, though, is ruined," Ty admitted.

"Can you get us out of here?" the demon asked anxiously.

"What, you want to go back to prison?" Ty asked, incredulous.

"No, of course I don't," the demon said, sounding exasperated. "However, it beats being trapped here."

"I can see that," Ty said, nodding. "Why couldn't you get yourself out of here?"

The demon grimaced. Even with so many teeth and such a huge mouth the expression was clear. "Look, I only hitched a ride here. My cousin Benny thought this would be a good place to stash me. He had no idea about those hell birds." The demon glared at the flock that had gathered just outside of the cave, like a miasma waiting to inflict them with doom. "I can't get out of here on my own. Okay?"

"Then let's go," Ty said. It didn't take him long to form a portal that led them straight to the bailiff's office, in the basement of the court of the Host.

Once his charge was booked, Ty nearly turned right around and headed for home. He deserved a good long soak, along with a large glass of whisky.

Something, though, made him look at the wanted board. He could excuse his behavior as professional interest, curiosity about where his next job might be coming from.

But he knew that something about the board raised his hunting instinct. Along with the hairs on the back of his neck.

Ty gulped when he saw the board.

There, in the middle, was a wanted poster with pictures of Lars Sorgenfreys in both his demon as well as human form.

Seemed that Lars had escaped prison.

With a sigh, Ty knew that his bath was going to be a long time in coming as he called Christine with the news.

CHAPTER ELEVEN

CHRISTINE DID NOT NORMALLY SWEAR. SHE FELT that using curse words was frequently a sign of a lack of imagination. Of course, there were some honestly creative curses, and Christine had always meant to practice some of those so that the correct *bon mot* would fall from her lips at exactly the right time.

However, just then, she felt like uttering every curse word she knew in every language she could think of. Even if she had to make some of them up herself.

Ty had just let her know that Lars had escaped from prison at least a week ago.

Why hadn't anyone notified her? Wasn't it the job of the Host and the court to keep all the races safe?

Ty hadn't been surprised that she hadn't known. Seemed that they probably wouldn't have said anything unless Lars hadn't been caught, say, after a month or so.

Did they really think that highly of their abilities to find the slippery demon? Christine had only barely managed to survive their last encounter.

She'd assured Ty that she didn't need him to come over or anything. The poor man sounded exhausted. She assumed that his latest prey had led him on quite a chase.

"I'll go see Nik tomorrow," Christine assured Ty before she hung up the phone. "He'll help me ensure that my protections are adequate." It would cost her, of course. Nik was first and foremost a businessman. He didn't do anything for free.

Tonight, well, tonight Christine was damned if she was going to change her plans. It was Saturday night, after all. She and Alanorin were going on a date.

Mud wrestling.

They'd gone to a couple of jello wrestling bouts. The green, lime jello had always bothered Christine's nose as well as her skin.

The mud, when it was done right, was actually better for Christine's tough hide. She'd joked with Tina about it being as good as a day at a spa. Tina hadn't seemed to appreciate the mud or the joke as much as Christine had.

Then again, Tina was merely human.

Christine really felt the need to get out and let loose with some of her pent up hostility tonight. Hopefully, Alan felt the same way, and that afterward they could both bask in the glow of their own "combat."

Although, sex with Alan wasn't as magical as it had once been. Christine had tried to communicate her needs, as much as she knew them. It felt to her as though Alan wasn't always interested in fulfilling them.

Was she being selfish? She honestly didn't know.

Tonight, Christine's human self wore a too-tight white camisole under a pink and baby-blue flannel shirt (it was Seattle, after all), along with skintight jeans and black combat boots. Her troll self wore merely a gray bikini top and cute boy shorts. She didn't bother with any sort of transformation, just throwing on an illusion spell to cover herself so that most who saw her were fooled.

She hurried to meet Alan at the meet, far up north, just off of Aurora Avenue in Shoreline. The area was slowly being gentrified, as there had at one point been hookers on every corner of this neighborhood. Asian markets and Halal restaurants were taking over what had once been preliminarily a Mexican neighborhood.

The portal she used was near the parking lot of a dive bar that sometimes had really good live music. The lot tonight was full of Harleys and other big bikes. Maybe she and Alan would have to stop by later for a beer or something, listen to some music before they headed back to her place.

Or maybe not. She winced as the first bad chord rang out from the open door of the bar. Whoever was in there needed to tune their instruments better, or to stop strangling that cat. She winced again at the next chord and hurried up the street.

The front part of the building Christine went to was still a gym. It had floor to ceiling windows across the front, so that people could be seen being virtuous. Mirrors lined the back. Useless treadmills and weight machines lined the walls. No free weights, which made Christine turn up her nose. Only then did she notice the smell of the gym—of human sweat and too little effort.

No one was stationed in the front part of the gym,

which made Christine a little concerned. Just anyone could walk in here. Even the reception desk was empty.

However, after she took a few steps into the room, she heard a lot of noise coming from the back, the roar of non-human voices echoing off hard, concrete walls.

This was the right place after all.

Alan stood just outside the door to the back, chatting easily with one of the orc bouncers. He looked good as a human, though Christine always preferred his troll form. He had long black hair that hung over his eyes, like a bad boy. His dark eyes, tiny nose, and thin lips gave him a mischievous look.

His human skin was dark colored, like hers, though a touch more tan, as if he had some Asian blood in him. He wore a green Army jacket that fit him snuggly across his broad shoulders, tight jeans, and black combat boots.

"Excuse me, gentlemen," Alan said, sliding away from the door and coming toward her. "Hello, darling," he said as he took her in his arms and kissed her, right there in front of everyone.

Christine wasn't really comfortable with the PDA. But she allowed it because she knew this was one of the ways that made Alan feel better here in the human plane, if he was allowed to touch her.

It was as though he needed a physical reminder that he wasn't here alone, by himself, even though he was standing right next to her and could see her.

"Hi, handsome," Christine said, smiling at him. She drew him closer for a quick hug, taking a deep breath of his scent.

That was one thing about Alan. He always smelled

right, like good solid earth and fresh air. Christine had dated a couple of other trolls before, but they'd never smelled right.

"I already registered us on the lists," Alan said as he took her by the hand and led her back toward the door. "We'll be in the fifth round."

"Great!" Christine said. She stopped before they reached the door, tugging on Alan's hand. "Can we talk for a moment before we go in there?"

Alan looked unhappy, but he said, "Sure. Let's go back up front."

He glanced over his shoulder at the two bouncers and rolled his eyes.

Christine bristled at the implication that of course, the woman wanted to *talk*.

Honestly, while she didn't care for human males, sometimes she wondered if she'd prefer dating one. At least a modern male who'd been brought up right. Troll males tended to be a lot more primitive. Which was sometimes lovely when it came to their sex life. Not so much in other areas.

Still, Christine held her head up high. These other wankers didn't need to know that one of the key generals of the demons had just escaped from prison and was up to no good.

At least not yet.

"You remember that demon I put into prison? Five years ago?" Christine asked.

Alan finally seemed to be catching a clue that Christine was not only serious, but a little bit freaked out.

"Yeah?" he said, seeming unsure.

Few trolls actually visited the human plane. In addition, not much news of Lars' capture had shown up in Trollville. Most of the news had been just about Princess Kizalynn returning.

"Lars—he's escaped from prison," Christine said.

Alan gave an appropriate reaction, his eyes grown wide. "Holy shit!" he said. "Do we need to go home? Right now?"

"No," Christine said firmly. "The bridge is as defended as it can be. Plus, he escaped over a week ago. If he were gunning for me, he already would have shown up. No, he must be up to something else. Something no good."

"You sure?" Alan asked. "I wouldn't want you to feel uncomfortable."

That was certainly an odd way to phrase that. "What do you mean?" Christine asked, puzzled.

"You know. Unsafe. I'd protect you," Alan assured her.

"Pfffft," Christine said. "I can protect myself."

Alan pulled himself up straighter at that. "I know," he said coldly. He glanced back at the door where the two orc bouncers still waited. They were occupied with the next pair who had come in. "Look, I need you to go easy tonight, okay?"

"What are you talking about?" Christine said. She had a sinking feeling of what it was that Alan was asking of her. She needed for him to spell it all out, so that she wouldn't be making a false assumption.

"I told the guys that you were a sure bet. To lose," Alan said.

"You what?" Christine said growling. She wasn't mad, not yet. But she was certainly inching up that incline.

"The odds were in favor of us winning," Alan said. "Now, you know that it would look funny if I bet against myself."

"So you bet for us, but now you're trying to make more money? By what, having me throw the first bout or something?" Christine said. She'd hit fuming at this point. Boiling angry was just around the corner.

Alan should *know* better. Christine wasn't a hothead, but she was a troll. It wasn't ever going to take much to get her riled up.

Particularly not with the week she'd had, with Dennis still scolding her for almost forgetting Father's Day, how Christine's hair still looked (making her feel like a poofy dog), how down Tina was about her magic and what a tragedy that would turn into if she *did* lose her magic, her own father finding out that he *did* have magic, and now Lars escaping.

Alan shrugged. "That was kind of the idea. If we went down the first couple of rounds, then made a grand comeback in the last."

"I won't do it," Christine said. "That isn't honest."

"And you're always all about being honest, right?" Alan asked archly.

"What are you talking about?" Christine said, confused.

"How long did it take you to tell me your true heritage?" Alan said. "That you were actually troll royalty?"

Christine sighed. "You're right. I should have told you sooner. I apologized for that." And she had, more than once. She just hadn't known how to bring it up! What was she supposed to do, introduce herself then say, "Oh, by the way, I'm also a princess? Next in line for the throne?"

"You've also always kept your magical abilities under wraps," Alan pointed out.

"That isn't anyone else's business," Christine countered. Besides, if she showed up all glowy, people would automatically know that she was royalty. For the most part, only troll royalty had any magic. So maybe she should next time, just so the other trolls would know.

But that was going to make it harder than the toughest granite to find anyone who really wanted to date her and not her position.

"So let's just lay it on the line, tonight," Alan challenged. "You and me. Let's see who's the better troll."

"I don't want to fight you," Christine said, a sinking feeling starting to roll through her belly. "I wanted to fight *with* you, together, against all comers."

"No," Alan said. "Not tonight. Let's just shake things up. Okay?"

Christine shook her head. Nothing good was going to come of this. Nothing.

However, if this was how Alan wanted to break up with her, then that was going to be on *his* head. Not hers.

———

BOXING MATCHES HAD BEEN HELD IN THE ROOM before tonight. The center ring had been replaced with a large children's wading pool. It was maybe fifteen feet in diameter, with an edge rising about a foot and a half off the floor. Good brown mud filled the bottom of the pool, leaving a rim of shocking blue.

Old-fashioned wooden risers circled the pond in the middle, to give those watching the fights a good view. The seats were already mostly packed with *kith and kin*—orcs, dwarves, brownies, pixies, dark elves, and other creatures who Christine was still trying to come up with a proper taxonomy for. (Again, why would *nobody* write anything down?)

Christine separated from Alan when they entered the room. He was going to make all the accommodations, get the lists changed, etc.

Of course, he wasn't about to change his bets. He would never bet against himself.

And maybe that had been part of the problem all along, that Christine wouldn't have bet against them as a couple, while he was only concerned with himself.

She went to sit on the benches opposite the door, scooching herself in between a group of pixies with their long, mis-jointed fingers and wicked teeth on the one side, and a pack of dwarves on the other. Both groups ignored her. Christine loosened her illusion slightly, making her face appear half-troll, half human, just so the others would feel more comfortable around her.

Like Tina, Christine was never comfortable in a crowd, though all of the beings here were *kith and kin*, which made it a lot more tolerable.

The first fight would be a couple of orcs. Both males, dressed in speedos (never a good look for anyone, no matter what race.) They came out of their corners, snarling as they stalked toward the mud-filled pool. Bright spotlights followed them. The crowd started yelling.

Christine compared the pair of them to Patrick, the orc she regularly boxed and wrestled with. Patrick was a shade taller, as well as thinner. His body was shaped by free weights and fighting. These two looked like gym rats, with pretty physiques instead of useful muscles.

The announcer came on the loudspeaker. Both orcs received a lot of cheers as well as boos. They strutted around the outside of the wrestling pool like the fake human wrestlers did.

Finally, the pretty boys, as Christine had come to think of the two orcs, climbed into the ring. The mud wasn't too thick, but it was slick. She could see that by how they adjusted their stances.

Without waiting for the announcer to officially start the bout, the first raced at the second, angrily growling. He slammed into his opponent with a high body check. The other orc fell backwards directly into the mud.

Wait. How did that even work? Christine knew the pressure points on a body. Striking someone in the chest, unless they were coming at you with speed, would *not* drop someone to the ground like that. They'd stumble back.

Something else was going on.

The two orcs taunted each other before grappling again. The mud was slippery and their tricks were easier to disguise. But Christine watched how they pulled their punches, fell without provocation, and got back up after the most dire of tumbles.

They were merely putting on a show. None of it was real.

Did none of the other beings watching see through these tricks? Or was the crowd in on it? Did they accept that it was a game?

Christine didn't know. She tried to peer at the faces of some of the *kith and kin* while at the same time not to stare too hard or give any offense. It was difficult as the sidelines were in shadow, and bright spotlights shone down on the participants.

She cursed her upbringing again. She'd never been around the other *kith and kin* enough to be able to read their facial expressions or body language clearly. She still struggled with some of the non-verbal cues of trolls. It was possibly why she kept failing at her relationships—she'd been unable to read what her partner was truly telling her.

However, it wasn't up to her to unmask these fighters.

She just needed to remember their names and their faces, and to never rely on them in the upcoming war.

Finally, the winner was declared. Though the announcer tried to incite someone else to come and fight the bad boy who'd just won, there were no takers.

Christine was tempted to take them up on it. However, she wasn't about to. She would end up shaming the fighter. And again, that wasn't her place.

Besides, she had her own bout coming up, one that she was approaching with deadly seriousness.

Then the second bout started, with two cat-like creatures who actually put on a good fight, not just a show.

When the winner from the first bout went back into

the ring for the next round, Christine watched more carefully. How was he telegraphing his moves? Or was it all choreographed?

Only this time, the orc was really fighting. And his opponent was good.

Either the first orc hadn't been as good at play acting or it had been a setup, to get the beings here to bet more as they were certain to be entertained.

Now, Christine was interested in meeting this orc, the one who was both an actor as well as a real fighter. Orcs weren't known for either their cleverness or for being sneaky.

Christine had a soft spot for all of that and more.

Finally, the fifth bout arrived. The announcer came on the speaker, introducing Alan first.

"And in the other corner, well aren't we honored tonight? It's Princess Kizalynn Linumok Te'Dur!"

Christine gasped. Why would Alan do that to her? Break her cover that way?

Alan stepped out of his corner and up to the ring, looking tall and proud of himself.

Wanker.

A spotlight revolved around the small space, shining on the crowd, as if trying to pick Christine out.

Slowly, Christine stood up. She didn't bother trying to hide that she'd been using a spell to disguise herself.

One moment, a troll-like woman stood in front of them.

The next moment, a troll herself was there.

The crowd gasped.

Oh, this was going to be priceless.

Christine stepped into the ring, dipping her hands into the mud, coating them thoroughly. She wasn't going to bother covering the rest of her body in it.

The fight was going to be over far too quickly for that.

Alan called out a taunt in trollish, "Your father is weak and smells of mead!"

Christine couldn't help but roll her eyes. "And *your* father likes human women," she said in reply.

A couple of gasps from the audience told her that at least some understood Trollish. It was a serious insult.

Alan narrowed his eyes. "You're not one to talk."

Christine shrugged. She couldn't help how she'd been brought up, as a changeling. It wasn't her fault. And anyone who thought that it was, was an idiot.

Like Alan.

Christine waited until Alan finished posturing. He bent over and growled at her, showing off his fangs.

Boy had never used them in battle now, had he?

Christine merely widened her stance and waited.

Without warning, Alan charged at Christine.

It seemed as though time slowed for her. The crowd grew silent. The smell of dirt and sweat and *anger* filled her nostrils.

Alan was slightly bent over, as if intending to tackle her into the mud.

He certainly wasn't moving fast enough to get the drop on her.

Christine timed her punch perfectly, striking Alan under the jaw with her powerful fist.

His own momentum carried him upwards.

Christine followed through with the punch, her fist rising to the ceiling.

Alan's eyes crossed from the impact. His body grunted from the force.

Then everything sped up again.

Alan's body flew back into the mud.

He rose up on his elbow and shook his head, moving his jaw around.

The crowd went wild.

With a loud growl, Alan launched himself at Christine, intending to take her down. Again.

She blocked his attempt with a foot to his face.

He was lucky that she was well trained. She could have just as easily broken his neck with that maneuver.

She slapped away every punch he threw at her, efficiently blocking them. Then she swept his legs out from under him, dropping him into the mud again.

The crowd cheered her on, though it wasn't as raucous as it had been.

Christine wasn't playing along, wasn't giving them a show, not how they'd been expecting. This was serious.

"Are you done?" Christine asked Alan after she did a second leg sweep and dropped his butt into the mud. He was coated from head to foot, while only Christine's hands and feet had mud on them.

"Never," Alan growled.

"Your choice," Christine told him.

As the entire evening had been—his choice of venue, his choice of the fight.

His choice for living his life without her.

When he came at her again, Christine had a punch combination all set. One to the stomach, one to the ribs, then the last, the hardest punch, to the side of his head.

She struck him with so much force that he spun around and ended up face first in the mud.

With one hand she pulled his shoulder up, leaving him face up so he wouldn't choke. Still passed out.

"And the winner is…Princess Kizalynn!" the announcer said over the speakers.

The crowd cheered until Christine held up her hands, indicating that she wanted to say something.

Christine had never been good at public speaking. She'd been a librarian, for goodness sakes, specifically so that she didn't have to ever talk with anyone.

She still waited until the crowd had mostly calmed down, when there was just shuffling noises in the background.

"My good beings," Christine said. "You saw this battle. You've been watching fights for a while now. But this is nothing, *nothing*, at all like what is almost upon you."

The crowd had grown entirely silent now.

Maybe Christine was getting better at this.

"War is coming. The Great War," she warned. "One of the chief demon generals just escaped his prison. He'll be coming for you. For me."

Christine looked around the room again, her gaze as cold as a winter's morn.

"Be prepared."

Later that evening, Christine laid back in her lovely clawfoot tub, filled with Epson salts, and had herself a good cry.

She had the feeling that, even given how truly awful this week had been—between Lars breaking out of prison, her father discovering he had magic, and her boyfriend breaking up with her—it was all about to get much, much worse.

CHAPTER TWELVE

Holy fuck.

Lars couldn't believe his eyes or his ears.

His plan *worked*. The demons in the field of battle before him were winning. All the reports were coming in with casualties on the other side.

It was a tiny pocket world, filled with fawns, creatures who were constantly confused with the satyrs. Instead of having the legs (and attitude) of a goat, they were a mix of deer and human. A little shy, but when cornered, they turned into fierce fighters.

No one was going to miss this little pocket plane or the fawns who'd resided in it. Not for a good long while. Possibly not until after the Great War had already started, though Lars didn't believe his luck would be that good.

His armies had all been carrying the corrupt corruption gems. The force of their will was overwhelming. The fawns had put up token resistance, but their lines had collapsed. Quickly.

Lars usually didn't put the magical power into his

wings that was necessary for him to achieve full flight. Normally, he glided or merely hopped.

This time, his armies needed to see their glorious general, to hear his bellowing cry, to feel their victory deep in their bones.

With a mighty push, Lars leaped off the ground. Even here in a pocket world, created by magic, it wasn't easy to obtain altitude. Still, he rose up, calling out their victory so everyone could hear. The demons below him raised up their bloodied snouts, looking up from their feasts of the fallen, and cheered.

Lars circled the battlefield. Off at the far end, some of the fawns still tried to run away, to seek refuge elsewhere. Demons loped after them, laughing at their enemy, rejoicing in their chase. Lars shouted orders down at them, telling them to speed it up.

It wouldn't do for any of the fawns to escape and go and warn the other worlds.

He already had demons set in place on the human plane who would kill any fawn before they made a full report to the Host.

It was too soon for his plans to be revealed.

Plans within plans.

Lars was ready, however, for when the slaughter that he and the other generals had released would be known.

Because by then, it would be far, far too late.

CHAPTER THIRTEEN

D ENNIS SAT ON HIS LEATHER COUCH IN HIS LIVING room, with none of the lights on, slowly drinking a beer. It wasn't completely dark. The shades weren't drawn on the windows in front of him, showing the lights of downtown Bellevue. Behind him, in the kitchen, the clock on the stove shone with a bright green light, as did the second clock on the microwave above it.

Down the hallway, the door to the bathroom was open, and the light from his electric toothbrush gave quite a bit of illumination. As did the light from his clock in the bedroom.

Dennis didn't normally sit in the dark, or the semi-dark, or whatever you'd call the light levels in his condo. He usually didn't drink beer alone, except on the occasional afternoon when he was by himself watching the game, or sometimes when he was unable to sleep and would turn on late-night TV, drink a beer and watch infomercials until he was tired enough to go back to bed.

In addition, Dennis didn't generally contemplate the

entirety of his life. One of his previous girlfriends had accused Dennis of being as introspective as a mud puddle.

She hadn't been completely wrong, but also, not completely right. The events over the course of the last five years had caused Dennis to become more reflective.

Finding out that there was magic in the world and whole societies of beings who weren't human living right beside you did that to a person.

Particularly after discovering that your sister was a troll. A princess troll. Troll royalty. And that your biological sister was one of the strongest magicians in the world.

That was all old news for Dennis, however.

Tonight, he needed to think about what it meant to be second fiddle.

No one liked to think of themselves as merely being the supporting cast. Everyone wanted to be the hero of their own tale.

But Dennis…well it had just been shoved in his face, yet again, that he wasn't the important one. He didn't have a Destiny, not like the others in his family.

He took another sip of his beer, making a face at how sour it had grown. Then again, he wasn't drinking to drink, otherwise he'd probably be drinking whisky or something harder. The beer was just something to do while he sat and thought.

Mostly.

The first insult had come when he'd discovered that Lars, his best friend for most of his life, was only hanging around Dennis so that he could keep track of Christine.

Since Dennis was in an honest mood tonight, he may

as well admit that while some of the things that Lars had said about his sister had rankled Dennis, too many of Lars' comments hadn't.

And what kind of big brother did that make Dennis?

He'd tried to make it up to her, this trollish sister of his, but he feared it would never be enough.

Then came the realization that Christine had a Destiny. Not only that, but his bio-sis, Tina, also had one.

No one had even bothered taking Dennis to the Oracles to see if he had a Destiny. He wasn't that important in the grand scheme of things.

Once Lars had finally been put into prison for a good long while, Christine had taken Dennis to Nik, as well as bargained for some time with Tina, to see if they could at the very least teach Dennis some magic.

But Dennis had the magical power of a used-up piece of gum. That is to say, none. Nada. Zip.

Magic ran in families. Now, Christine was a powerfully magica; troll because she was a princess. While Tina was magical just on her own.

There had to be *someone* in the Tuckerman family who was magical. Tina wouldn't occur in a vacuum. Magic might skip a generation, though normally it didn't.

No one had suspected that *Dad* might have magic. He certainly hadn't registered as magical earlier. Seemed that the constant exposure to magic may have triggered his latent tendencies.

The same exposure to magic hadn't changed Dennis in the least.

He liked to tease Christine that he'd been "born ready," an expression from a bad 1970s action flick.

He wasn't, though. Not really. Nothing could have prepared him for magic and demons and trolls. While his job continued normally, hanging out with his friends had been slowly evolving as well.

Most of his buddies were now either married off or already engaged. Dennis didn't even have a steady girlfriend. He hadn't been able to keep any.

Again, always playing second fiddle, permanently in the "friend zone" with most of his exs.

Tonight, it had all come crashing in on him when he'd started thinking about the consequences of Dad having magic, of the war about to start again, how Christine wouldn't have much time or even use for him.

He was merely human. There wasn't anything he could do against a magical demon attack, except to act as a distraction and maybe get himself killed before Christine could come and save him.

Second fiddle.

He took another swallow of sour beer. It matched the sour taste the words left behind.

Tomorrow, he was certain he'd see things differently. He'd come up with yet another grand scheme to help his trollish sister, or the various worlds, during the course of the war.

Maybe tomorrow he could make a significant contribution.

Tonight…tonight he'd just stay in his spot, accept his fate, and not try to push beyond it.

Second fiddle.

But at least he had a great view of the action from here.

CHAPTER FOURTEEN

VERN LOOKED WITH INTEREST AROUND MALCOM'S house. He'd been in Christine's practice room, but that had been built for a large troll swinging an ax. The rest of Christine's sprawling underground home had been filled with books and knickknacks, much like Christine's human apartment had been.

She considered it comfortable. Vern felt claustrophobic in that warren, but he never said anything except how proud he was of his daughter. Both his daughters.

Because he was.

Malcom's house was located up in the Queen Anne neighborhood. Not one of the expensive mansions, or one of the older craftsmen, but a nice brick rambler built in the 50s. The yard was tiny but immaculate, the grass carefully tended, the cherry blossoms all blown away, even from the cracks in the sidewalk.

The house itself felt warm and lived in, the perfect combination.

"Want some coffee?" Malcom asked as he welcomed Vern in. The usual greeting for anyone in Seattle.

"Sure," Vern said. "If it wouldn't be that much bother," he added hastily.

Malcom laughed, a warm expression that just made Vern believe that everything was going to be all right.

Malcom wore yet another argyle vest, this time knit out of yellow with black lines and baby-blue highlights, along with gray slacks and house slippers. Vern felt decidedly underdressed in his red sportswear T-shirt, jeans, and flipflops. But he couldn't seem to motivate himself to wear much else. It just didn't seem worth the bother anymore, though he'd never been what you would have called a clothes horse.

"Making coffee isn't a bother," Malcom assured Vern. "I was just about to make myself another cup."

Malcom led Vern through the living room (full of wood and books as well as a lovely fireplace in the corner and comfortable chairs in front of it) and into the kitchen. It was just as welcoming. White-painted cabinets covered two of the walls, while windows overlooking the backyard filled a third wall, and doorways leading into the room as well as to the downstairs took up most of the last one.

Black and white tile covered the countertops that ran between a large, brand new, stainless steel sink, a modern black gas stove, with a matching refrigerator tucked into the far corner.

"How long have you had this place?" Vern asked. The kitchen felt cozy, particularly with the smell of buttered toast that lingered in the air.

"Almost twenty-five years, now," Malcom said. He

poured water into a pot and set it on the stove, then got out a French press. "The neighborhood has changed quite a bit."

Vern snorted. "Kind of an understatement, right?" he guessed.

Malcom nodded. "True enough." He measured coffee beans into a tall cylindrical hand-grinder.

"Huh," Vern said, indicating the hand-grinder. "Why would you do that by hand?"

Malcom gave him a sly grin. "And not by magic?"

Vern shrugged. That had been his question in part. He didn't know that much about magic, despite having two daughters who were active practitioners.

And wasn't that a kick? Daughters who had power like that?

"Now, I can't tell you much about troll magic," Malcom warned. "To start with, trolls are rare on the human plane. And in addition, not many trolls have magic."

Vern nodded. He already knew that.

"As for human magic, as far as I can tell, it operates on a whole different set of criteria. Christine uses the elements for her power, right?" Malcom asked as he finished grinding the coffee and poured the grounds into the press.

"Yup," Vern said. "She has some sort of elementals, of fire, water, earth, and air, who make up her magic. They, in turn, get their power from the actual elements of fire, water, earth, and air." He was proud that he knew at least that much.

"Fascinating," Malcom said. "You'll have to tell me

what you know about it later." He sounded like an eager scholar, looking for the topic of his next thesis.

Malcom lifted the lid on the pot sitting on the stove, checking the temperature of the water. "One thing to remember—all magic has a cost. It might not be obvious at first. But you can't create something out of nothing. The power and the materials, or even the essence, comes from somewhere."

"So where does Tina get her power from?" Vern asked. He'd never really thought through the mechanics of magic, just that it was nifty keen that Tina was so strong.

"Some of it comes from the elements, like Christine's magic. Some of it leaks through from the other planes. And some of it comes just from Tina's self."

"Cool," Vern said. "Does she get to pick and choose? So, say, she's feeling kind of yucky, can she still do magic, just stealing it from somewhere else?"

"It doesn't really work that way," Malcom said as the water in the kettle on the stove finally reached the perfect temperature. "What Tina would do, if she were feeling yucky, as you so aptly put it, would be to choose a different spell. She would have learned as she practiced which spells put more strain on her personally, versus the spells that didn't."

"How does the magic get renewed?" Vern asked as Malcom poured the water over the grounds, then set a timer. Vern approved. He really liked a good French press, and Malcom seemed to be an expert at this, turning it into a ritualized art form.

"What do you mean?" Malcom asked.

"If a spell sucks away some of the magic from one of

the pocket worlds, how does that world recover that magic? Does it just regenerate it? Is there some special formula for renewing the worlds?"

Vern knew he sounded like some sort of hippy, but he'd never really cared.

"There are theories, of course, about how it happens," Malcom said. "But no one knows for certain. Just be assured that we aren't sucking the other worlds dry of magic. It continues to renew itself."

"Kind of like magic?" Vern said with a wink.

"Exactly," Malcom said, grinning. "But that won't be where we start when it comes to learning magic," he assured Vern. "We'll need to start at the basics and work our way up from there."

"When did you first discover you had magic? And became a teacher?" Vern asked. "And thank you, by the way, for volunteering to teach me."

"I don't take on many students these days," Malcom said. "I'm semi-retired, like you. However, teaching an adult is *always* easier than teaching kids who think they already know it all."

"The last time I probably thought I knew it all was when I was a snot-nosed kid," Vern said.

Malcom poured them both cups of coffee, then held his out to clink his cup against Vern's. "Here's to never returning to the foolish days of our youth," he said solemnly.

"Here, here," Vern agreed.

"Now, to answer your question, I was told by my Mammy, my grandmother, back when I was a little thing, maybe five or six," Malcom said. "She was known as a powerful witch in the community. So she started training me early. However, turned out that I never had that much power."

"Why's that?" Vern asked, curious.

Malcom shrugged as he added a spoonful of honey to his coffee, then topped it off with cream. Vern took his black, as always. He'd considered it personally a shame for someone to ruin a good cup by adding things to it.

"My mom always said it was because I was a spiteful thing, contrary by nature, and never doing what was expected of me," Malcom said with a big grin.

Vern raised his cup to that, too. "Been accused of that many a time."

"Honestly, being selfish…that's just the nature of magicians," Malcom said seriously.

"So I've heard," Vern said, just as serious.

Malcom led him into a study that was just as comfortable as the rest of the house. A large, roll-top desk was pushed up against the far wall, with a glass-fronted bookshelf sitting on top of it. More bookshelves covered one wall, filled with books that Vern could smell were ancient. A curiously blank spot stood between the two windows, given how every other wall was covered. Gauzy white curtains hung over the tall, skinny windows that overlooked the side yard.

At least half a dozen chairs filled the small space. Malcom grabbed the captain's chair that was in front of the desk, then wheeled it over to one of the wingback chairs that stood in front of the first window.

"Please, sit," Malcom said.

Vern gulped. He was ready for this. Really. He sat and

then tried to stay still, not fidget like a two year old who's had too much sugar.

He took another sip of his excellent coffee, setting the mug down on a coaster on the end table beside him.

"Okay," Vern said, spreading his hands wide and pressing them down on his thighs. "Do your worst."

Malcom gave him a sly smile. "Oh, I intend to."

Wait a minute. Were Malcom's eyes suddenly glowing?

Vern felt himself falling forward, out of his chair.

Then darkness.

VERN FOUND HIMSELF SITTING BACK IN THE wingback chair in Malcom's study. He reached for and took a sip of his ice-cold coffee, still delicious even though it was no longer fresh.

"What…happened?" Vern asked. "I remember walking into here. Then…nothing." He felt very unsettled, missing all those hours.

Yet, at the same time, he still felt as though he'd learned something. What exactly, he couldn't say. But he felt more full now, than he had earlier. He suppressed a yawn. And tired.

"It's a perfectly normal reaction to not remember the details of your first lessons," Malcom explained. "You've considered yourself a regular, mundane human being your entire life. When faced with the new reality, your conscious self shuts down. In time, after your unconscious comes to accept your powers, you'll start to remember these first few lessons. I see it all the time."

"Even with children?" Vern asked. Everything Malcom said sounded reasonably enough. Yet…

"Not as frequently with them," Malcom admitted. "It still happens."

"So Tina—"

"Took to her lessons like a duck to water," Malcom said. "There was no stopping that girl, no holding her back from her magic."

"Good," Vern said. He didn't feel like a duck, or water, or much of anything at all. Another wave of tiredness washed over him, and he was unable to stifle a yawn.

"And that's perfectly normal too," Malcom said. "Most of the kids go for a nap as soon as they finish their lessons."

"That sounds like good advice," Vern said as he slowly stood up. "Gosh diddly winkers, I'm tired."

"Go home. Sleep. We'll meet again next week," Malcom told him.

"Thank you," Vern said. Though he knew that people who performed magic didn't like being touched, he still held out his hand for Malcom to shake.

Malcom gamely took Vern's hand and gave it a strong pump. "It was my pleasure," he said, sounding sincere.

It wasn't until Vern was driving back through Seattle, using city streets to make his way back to Madison Park, that he realized how strongly he felt the magic inside of him, as if he could have just flown back home. Despite his exhaustion, Vern felt himself grinning and singing a cheerful song about being a king.

Though he didn't remember much of the morning, how he felt now would surely make up for it.

CHAPTER FIFTEEN

Buddy had insisted on written reports from Lars, just because he knew how irritated it would make the younger demon.

Lars would have *much* preferred meeting with Buddy in person, just so he could brag about his results, or because he thought he'd be able to actually lie about his failures.

They always did, not realizing that as a prince of hell, Beelzebub had kind of been around at the time of the *invention* of the lie. May have contributed a little something to it.

So he didn't even need to be in the same room in order to smell one, even a little white one.

Buddy sat in his office, bare feet up on the desk, looking over the report that Lars had sent him. The room was only big enough for a full-sized demon or three. Buddy had an old desk carved out of marble, then enchanted so that (most) demon slime didn't automatically eat its way through the rock. It was a stark white with black streaks running through it, with some flecks of gold in the veins.

One of the things Buddy liked about his desk, besides the fact that it was fucking solid (and he had actually fornicated on it, more than once), was that it retained a natural coolness, even in Hell. He frequently placed his feet on it to cool them off, particularly after spending an afternoon walking on hot coals while he met with some of the other demons. (The coals served as a distraction, being too hot for some demons, really comfortable for others, and therefore always giving Buddy the upper hand since he could ignore the heat until later.)

The rest of the room was more mundane. Really, the huge iceberg of a desk was the most impressive thing in there. He had some limestone stalactites reaching down from the ceiling, dripping water sometimes on those unfortunate enough to be made to stand there. Unlike the throne room, Buddy went for more modern here: walls made out of solid concrete tiles, gray and black; floor made out of poured concrete (that also stayed cool most of the time); window portals that looked out on the domain of Hell, so Buddy could keep an eye on his workers as well as take a break now and again to watch souls being tortured.

The only chair in the room was the one Buddy sat on. Really, if he called some other demon in here, it wasn't going to be an extended affair. (Okay, so maybe there were a few exceptions to that, but then again, they'd actually been affairs.)

Lars' report contained all of the detailed minutia of a

dense year-end business statement from a company trying to hide their falling profits.

Except that…Lars was reporting victory, as far as Buddy could tell.

Lars had completely wiped out ninety percent of the fawns, and was busily tracking the rest across the planes and killing them off as well.

Buddy got a tingling feeling inside at the thought of an actual xenocide. They hadn't had one of those in centuries.

Of course, Lars had to brag about how his plans had worked, how successful the armies had been carrying the corrupted corruption spell gems (CCSG for short, which was not to be confused by just corruption spells—CS—as well as corrupted corruption spells—CCS.)

Buddy found himself torn. He wanted to win the Great War. Lars had just taken a nice step forward in their plans. Buddy sincerely hoped that Lars would be as successful with his next battle, and the one after that.

However, Buddy still wasn't sure that he wanted to be shown up by such a young whippersnapper. Lars was still in his first body. Older demons would eventually swap out their previous physical form for a newer one, generally by swallowing the soul of the former inhabitant.

Buddy could claim credit for everything. He probably would, eventually.

But did he really want Lars to win? Buddy was pretty comfortable here in his spot in Hell. The other princes of Hell would grumble just as much when Lars demanded his own offices down here. And if he won the war, they'd have to grant him the space.

No matter how much of the spotlight Buddy stole for himself, eventually Lars would have to be recognized.

Or else that stupid punk would try to start a revolution in Hell.

More than one demon had gotten a good start that way. Additionally, Lars would already have a following, particularly if he was successful at the war.

He might win and own Hell if Buddy wasn't careful.

So Buddy decided to set his own PR machine into motion, making sure that while Buddy's name was mentioned, Lars' was more prominent.

It was just safer to start pumping Lars up now, impressing everyone with how important Lars was to the war effort, how the demons might have a chance because of Lars and the risks he'd taken.

Because in the end, when Lars failed and fell, he wouldn't be taking Buddy with him.

CHAPTER SIXTEEN

Nik looked over the ingredient list that the demon had handed him. The demon herself was as tall as a giant, her head nearly brushing against the eighteen-foot ceilings in Nik's shop. She wasn't any particular class of demon, at least not as far as Nik could tell. If anything, he'd classify her as upper middle class, from a higher born family who still had to work to get ahead. She had the bony structure favored by them, with the flesh flayed off her torso and back. Her hands barely worked, as the ligaments seemed to be over stretched. He wouldn't be surprised if she could bend her hand back and touch her elbow without really trying.

Her skin was at least dark enough to hide some of her more obvious sores and wounds. And her teeth had mostly rotted out, leaving her with a sweeter smile than she probably found comfortable. She had that sour cabbage smell that Nik would bet turned off other demons.

"Why are you looking for sweetened poisoned hemlock?" Nik asked, curious.

"None of your business, shopkeeper," the demon replied.

Did she think it was an insult to call Nik by his chosen profession?

Probably. Demons thought that any being who wasn't a demon was naturally beneath them.

"Just curious about it, that's all," Nik said. "Been seeing a lot of demons coming through and asking for ingredients used primarily in human spells."

She shrugged and didn't seem inclined to satisfy his curiosity.

He wasn't going to ask why more demons were coming here and asking for demon spell ingredients. They had their own suppliers and shops. He generally catered more to humans and the *kith and kin*.

Were the demons just using up that much material that their own suppliers could no longer meet the demands?

Why?

Nik returned back to the list. "Sure, I can get you all of these." He pointed to the virgin's tears, pressed daisies, and frog tails. "These I'm going to have to order. They'll be here tomorrow. Some of the other items though…they're going to take longer."

"Can't you get in anything today?" the demon growled.

At least she didn't try to press her influence against him. Maybe the few who had tried had warned the others about how quickly that would get them refused service.

More likely, most of them did try to influence Nik and just weren't strong enough for him to even notice.

"I have at least half your list already in stock," Nik said. "Do you want to purchase those items now, then come back and get the rest in, say, a week's time?"

"No, I do not want to have to make two trips," the demon snarled. "Can't you at least deliver?"

"Certainly I can! It's just that there's an additional fee involved," Nik explained. He quoted her a price, double to what he usually charged.

"All right," the demon said, not even bothering to bargain. "I want it all delivered here." She flipped the list around, stole a pen from the top of Nik's counter (Nik knew she'd never return it) and wrote down the coordinates for one of the pocket worlds. "Need it all there."

"If you'll wait for just a moment, I'll gather up the ingredients I already have on hand," Nik said.

"No, deliver them all there," the demon insisted.

She didn't seem very interested in the price bargaining that followed, only knocking Nik's starting bid down by about a third, instead of the two thirds that he was expecting.

"Is there a name I should put on the parcels?" Nik asked as he gave the demon her change.

"Matilda," the demon said. "And Lars."

The way she said it made shivers run down Nik's spine, truly an impressive feat.

Not much was capable of disgusting him. However, the way she's said his name implied just how deeply she was enamored with Lars. She sounded like a Korean school girl mentioning the name of her favorite singer of a boy band, her secret internet boyfriend.

It was a tone full of admiration, lust, and manic devotion.

How had Lars gotten himself a groupie?

Was Matilda not bargaining with Nik so much because she was paying for this herself? And wanted the bragging rights of how much she'd paid for Lars and his cause? Compared to the others in his entourage?

Matilda didn't bother even leaving the shop through the regular portal, but disappeared rudely in a puff of smoke.

Nik was so glad that his own sense of smell had never been transferred with his consciousness to his wooden body.

He called up winds to blow away the stench and smoke that would be certain to disturb whoever came into the shop next. Then he started to collect the ingredients that were on hand, letting his hands do the work while his brain kept gnawing at the conundrum that was before him.

Nik would sell to anyone. And he *never* talked about the purchases made by his customers. That would not be ethical. He believed strongly in their privacy. And if he did ever break his neutrality, he suspected he'd get a visit from an angel.

However.

Was there some way to at least alert the humans that the demons were preparing themselves for all-out war? Could he somehow tell the Host? How could he let someone, anyone, know, without violating the principles that were the foundation of his being?

He would make money no matter who won the next Great War.

It would just be a much more pleasant experience if it wasn't the demons.

CHAPTER SEVENTEEN

Ty turned around in the tiny, rock-strewn pocket world, sniffing for all his might. All his nose could find was the smell of sunbaked rock and the leading edge of the rain that was due in later that afternoon.

Damn it! He'd lost the trail. Again.

When Lars had broken out of prison, of course the other demons guarding him hadn't reported it right away. They'd probably thought that maybe they could find him, bring him back in, and perhaps pretend that it hadn't happened at all.

Only when the regular Host who audited the demons showed up the following week was it reported.

Then the Host had sat on the information for a while. Ty didn't know what bureaucrat had decided that it was better to hide the news rather than act on it. He did know that he was likely to string the bastard up if he ever met them.

Now, the trail was *cold*. It hadn't taken much persuasion for Ty to get himself assigned to the case, though it was offering a suspiciously low bounty for someone like Lars.

Maybe the Host realized just how dangerous Lars would be when he got cornered, and figured that they'd pay out in hospital and healing costs, and so didn't want to offer a lot of money for his recapture.

Or maybe there was some other conspiracy going on, a cooperation occurring between the Host and the demons, that Ty didn't want to think about. Not without driving himself absolutely batshit nuts.

Instead, Ty focused on the trail and finding Lars.

The Host had actually provided Ty with access to the prison that Lars had been held in. Ty had brought all of his gear: powders that would react to all types of magic, not just demon magic; crystals that would glow in the presence of hidden portals or pockets of goods; as well as the giant mechanical sniffer that he wore on his back, which had reminded more than one person of those industrial backpacks that ghostbusters had used.

The Host had also provided Ty with a deadening spell, so that he wouldn't be fully aware during his time in Hell. It was a mixed blessing.

On the one hand, Ty hated how much the spell muffled his sight, hearing, sense of smell, even taste.

On the other hand, being able to forget actually visiting Hell was a blessing that Ty wasn't about to turn down. Hell was the only place where Ty's control of the beast within was threatened.

The place was too damned hot, while the ground was too cold, a feat that only a demon could manage. The guards had already put another demon into the cell that had been inhabited by Lars. (Were they trying to cover up their mistakes? Or spoil the path and any evidence?)

Ty spent the morning there, using every powder, spell, and trick that he'd learned to figure out what had actually happened.

First of all, those *idiots* had let Lars obtain human form. It was probably in the official report, the one that Ty had not been permitted to read. But the traces in the cell were obvious. A human-like creature had resided there for a while.

The guards—two huge, horse-faced guards who seemed genuinely upset about what had happened on their watch—eagerly answered every question Ty had, even about the frog-like demon that Lars had summoned as a distraction.

"But there was more," Ty said as he prowled the cell. The traces were difficult to pinpoint, like trying to find the delicate footprints left behind by a dinosaur after a rave had been held on the excavation site. "There had to be a pocket here, someplace, where he hid all the ingredients."

The guards looked at each other and extravagantly shrugged their shoulders.

Which meant they knew exactly what Ty was talking about, having either thought of it themselves or been told about it after the fact, and now they were going to play dumb.

It didn't matter. Ty had learned all he needed to know.

Lars hadn't gone crazy while he'd been imprisoned. Instead, he'd gone where few demons ever went, deep inside himself, where he plotted and planned. The pockets where Lars had hidden his materials were at least a year old. Demons weren't known for their long-term thinking. Yet, that was exactly what Lars had been doing.

Ty wasn't going to like finding out the details of Lars' schemes, that much he knew.

———

FROM HELL, TY FOLLOWED THE TRAIL THROUGH HALF a dozen pocket worlds. Lars hadn't spent much time in any of them. He was obviously trying to muddle the trail.

Which Ty could appreciate. He kept finding then losing the trail. He honed his senses to detect a single rock out of place, the thinnest of scent trails, the slightest tremor of the magical sphere.

Now, Ty stood on a tiny pocket world, barely big enough to contain a single rock island. Mists surrounded it, hiding the other inhabitants of the world. If Ty stared hard enough, he saw figures in the mist, beings that he really didn't want to see. They hissed at his presence, sending chill, foreboding winds down his spine and ruffling the fur on his face, but they hadn't attacked.

Yet.

Ty *knew* that Lars had stepped through here. However, he'd probably only stayed long enough to call up another portal to someplace else.

How had Lars been able to skip so quickly from one world to the next? It was difficult to form a portal to someplace you'd never been before. Had Lars really traveled to all these locations at one point?

Or did he have an accomplice?

Ty took a moment to retune his senses, then cursed himself again.

Right there, in front of his nose, was a second demon scent, different than Lars'. If Ty retraced his steps, he was certain that in many of the locations he'd traveled through there would be different additional demon scents.

Ty had been so focused on Lars that it hadn't occurred to him that there might be traces of other demons. Or if there were other traces of demons, they were only a distraction.

For Ty and the other races he was familiar with, portals worked going from place to place.

Was it possible for a demon to create a portal to travel from person to person?

That would actually explain the behavior of the demons who Ty frequently chased. They frequently had a brother, sister, or cousin who traveled with them, or that they traveled to go see.

Ty stood lost in thought for a moment. Yes. Almost every account he'd heard of, when a demon had recounted their travel, had been about visiting someone with a portal.

They rarely talked about visiting a place.

Damn it! Now Ty was going to have to rethink his entire approach to demon hunting.

In the meanwhile…the mists had moved closer to the shore. Evidently they were more cautious about a stationary creature than one who was moving.

Ty followed the trail of the second demon straight to where the portal leading away from the island had been formed.

Now, was there only one? Had Lars gone through that one? Or had he formed his own?

Ty couldn't guess. He was going to take it a little easier on himself for the moment, though, and follow the more obvious trail.

If it tuned into yet another dead end, he could always come back here and see if he could tease out where Lars had actually gotten to.

Because at the end of the day, it didn't matter how many trails went cold on Ty.

He'd track down each and every one of them until he found his charge.

Ty stepped into a green world. Surprised, he held himself still as he looked around. Tall trees surrounded him. Dappled sunlight came through the branches. He heard the song of robins, the clicking of juncos, and the chittering of squirrels. Soft, fragrant breezes blew among the branches, tossing around the light at his feet.

Trails led through the underbrush of ferns. Pine trees lent their scent to the air. Maples, oaks, elms, and others grew wild.

Ty kept looking up, worried that perhaps some large cat or other creature was about to leap down and attack him. Nothing tracked him through the trees, however, other than the blue sky and sunshine.

This wasn't a demon world. Yet, Ty had followed a demon here. When he lifted his head and focused his nose, he caught the scent of a large group of demons who had passed through the area. It wasn't a fresh scent, maybe a few days old—possibly as much as a week. The rank smell momentarily overwhelmed his nose. He gagged, shaking his head, trying to clear his senses.

What was this world? And why had the demons come here?

Ty took two more steps, nearly tripping over a fallen log across the center of the path.

Then the scent of death rose up and he turned back.

It wasn't a brown log laying there, but a fawn. Its dead eyes still looked terrified. It had been shot in the back with a spell that had burned through its body, exiting out the front.

Had this fawn just had the misfortune of being in the wrong place at the wrong time? Had it been skipping merrily along this path when the demon—or demons— had appeared?

Ty hurried on, this time stepping more carefully.

He came across more dead fawns, over half a dozen of them. He could easily follow the scent of death.

They'd all been killed a while ago. Not weeks ago, but certainly days.

Why had no one come for the bodies? Tended to them and given them last rites?

Ty's fur was black, as was his face. Yet he could feel himself blanch and grow pale when he finally made his way out of the forest and into the small village.

Fawns were barely three feet tall, a shy race that kept to themselves. Tiny thatched huts ran along either side of the trail that had now widened into a dirt road, big enough for a wheeled cart.

Everyone in the village was dead.

No one had been spared by the demons. Babies as well as ancient fawns had all been killed. Many still bore the frenzy of battle, even in their endless sleep, with broken weapons in their hands and despair in their eyes.

What had the fawns done to the demons to rate such an attack? And why hadn't their natural magical abilities protected them? He should be finding more evidence of a fight, but it was as if the fawns had been so overwhelmed they hadn't taken out a single demon.

After poking around for a short while, Ty realized that the demons hadn't taken any prisoners. That surprised him. Demons liked torture. The fawns would have been particularly susceptible. Why had they all been killed instead?

Had all the demons left the pocket world of the fawns? Ty didn't think so, though it was difficult to distinguish the scent of a living demon from the army that had passed through.

He needed to explore this world and figure out what had happened. What the demons were up to.

Before another world (and its people!) suffered a similar fate.

CHAPTER EIGHTEEN

Christine wasn't sure what Ty meant by the text message he'd sent the evening before.

Be ready to fight tomorrow morning

Fight whom? Or what? Had Ty heard about the failed wrestling match with her ex? Though she didn't think that Ty had thought much of Alan.

Or had he heard about her considerable failure with Jose the orc? While Jose was sympathetic to her cause, he was more interested in what he could get out of her, rather than selflessly joining her eventual fight against the demons.

Christine had been disappointed, but she had difficulty judging just how much of a failure it was. She'd been recruiting for the last five years, and had built up quite an army.

Was it enough? How many beings did she need for the war? Twenty? One hundred? One thousand? How many demons would they be facing? How many fronts and battles would be run simultaneously? She knew that it was considered a weakness that she was allowing her enemy to choose the battleground. She didn't want to challenge the demons and get them to attack. What if she lost?

So while Christine was frustrated by the lack of details in Ty's text, that morning she still dressed in her version of the king's guard outfit: a solid blue jacket reinforced with steel plates and enough magic to encourage weapons to slide off, tough breeches that would also take quite a beating, along with heavy black combat boots. She debated wearing the peaked metal helmet, gold instead of silver, and in the end slung it around her neck. Hat hair notwithstanding, it was better for her to protect her head.

Of course, she had her huge ax tied to her back, a smaller sword on her left side, and the traditional bag of sharp rocks on the right.

When she felt Ty's presence up above, beside the bridge, she gracefully rose to the surface.

Ty was similarly attired, wearing a sleeveless vest with rings of metal sewn across it, trousers with metal plates sewn into them, and stiff boots. He also wore a metal helmet that had holes carved out of the top so that his ears could poke through. (Not that Christine still considered it a failure of the entire Troll race that while they had pointed ears, they had no control over them and couldn't swivel them like a dog's. She'd even tried several illusion spells so that it looked as though she could, but none of them had ever worked properly.)

"Good," Ty said, nodding at her outfit. "I'm glad you're prepared."

Christine stiffened at Ty's gruff voice. The demon hunter didn't sound scared, not exactly. No, more like raggedly determined, like a dog who'd chased his prey down to the earth only to have them vanish into thin air.

"Where are we going?" Christine asked as Ty started conjuring a portal. "Who are we fighting?"

"We're going to the world of the fawns," Ty said. His voice carried weird grim overtones. "And if we're lucky? No one. If we're not lucky? Demons."

CHRISTINE WASN'T SURE WHY TY HADN'T GIVEN HER more warning, telling her that they were about to go to where the fawns had been slaughtered. Had he been hoping that the shock would provoke more action from her? Didn't he realize that she'd been visited at least once a year by fawns, usually shyly going on vacation, their human illusions firmly in place? She'd always made time for them, finding a quiet corner of the Arboretum for them to sit in as they acclimated to the human plane.

A single dead fawn would have prompted her into action.

The mass slaughter of every fawn they ran across? Christine could no longer contain her growls, though she tried to hold them under her breath after Ty had asked her for silence more than once.

The world was lovely. It reminded her of Seattle on its best days, when it was sunny but not too hot, green and full of life.

There wasn't any way to bring the fawns back.

Christine knew that with each passing day, the pocket world of the fawns would lose more and more of its magic, until it was drained of color and air. It might turn into a hunk of useless rock, a barren wasteland, or it might collapse and disappear altogether.

Ty followed trails that Christine could barely discern through the trees and the underbrush, avoiding the main trails. Though the paths weren't much larger than two rutted trails running side by side, big enough for a small cart to be dragged along.

They passed several small villages before they finally came to the largest town, at least according to Ty and the maps he told her about. It was a walled place, though the ramparts were made of dirt, not stone. Most of the houses hidden behind the wall were similar enough to the ones in the villages, round and made of wood, with conical thatched roofs.

However, as a sign of how rich this place actually was, the wooden homes now frequently had beautiful carvings on the walls, or in some places, designs that had been etched in the wood with a controlled beam of fire. A river ran beside the main road, where fish still jumped and swam.

Off in the distance, toward the center of the town, a fire raged.

Ty tried to stay downwind of the smoke.

Christine coughed more than once, until Ty turned and glared at her. Then she tried to stay silent, particularly when she wanted to gag at the scent of roasting flesh. It almost smelled like venison. Almost. But it had a flavor of long pork as well, a scent that Christine wasn't ever likely to forget.

The sound of demons arguing came to them on the wind. Ty and Christine shared a look, then Christine drew out her ax and Ty unsheathed a long, wickedly curved sword.

Christine knew she should be horrified by what was around her, but she'd already grown numb. She also knew that she shouldn't be looking forward to any sort of fight with the demons, though she kind of was.

Any damage she inflicted on the demons remaining on this world would neither bring the gentle fawns back nor truly avenge their deaths.

The other reason Christine was looking forward to the battle was because she was curious how Ty handled that sword. It was a professional interest. Not that she was spoiling for a fight. Really.

"So what's the plan?" Christine asked quietly, coming up and whispering almost in Ty's ear.

He glanced at her, then back toward the direction the bulk of the smoke was coming from. "We need answers," Ty said.

Christine tried watching his mouth as he said the words, then quickly realized that was useless, as Ty's snout wasn't actually doing the speaking, that the words were spoken aloud using magic.

"Why the demons attacked the fawns?" Christine guessed. "And why they're cleaning up after themselves, burning the bodies?"

Did the whys matter? Not to her. What she wanted was revenge.

"Yes. Everything they're up to," Ty said.

"You think they're just going to tell us?" Christine asked. "Even if we capture one of them?"

Ty rocked his head back and forth. "Demons are kind of stupid. Particularly minions, the kind left behind to do cleanup work. They can be tricked into revealing more than they realize."

"Oh," was all the reply that Christine had. She hadn't thought of that.

Then again, she was a troll, and they weren't known for their sneakiness.

After Ty gave her a sharp nod, Christine moved out in front of Ty before they continued down the street. It wasn't that Christine was a better hunter—she adamantly was not—but they didn't really need hunting skills at this point. Where the demons were standing was obvious.

However, Christine was a *lot* tougher than Ty. Than any human, dwarf, or orc. Hell, she was tougher than most trolls by this point. Hopefully, tougher than the demon minions as well.

She'd been turning herself into a *bad-ass warrior princess* (as Dennis had called her) for a reason.

Now, it was time to reap the benefits of all that training.

They stalked forward silently. At least most of the dead fawns had been picked up by this point, though their blood still lay splashed against the cobblestone road, highlighting the carvings on the walls, as well as spilled onto the beautiful roses still humming with bees.

Around the corner lay a large town square. A huge

bonfire burned in the center of it. Three demons were arguing before the burning pyre.

The demons were what Christine would consider the minion variety. They were shorter than Lars or the upper class demons, and more, well, normal looking. They resembled corrupted men and women rather than creatures of nightmare. They had the usual pus, sores, and warts of all demons, though at least one had the stubs of bat wings reaching up from her back, offsetting the pointy breasts on the other side.

The other two were grossly male, with huge penises hanging down almost to their knees. They had the look of slobbering dogs, though with sharp snouts, more like hyenas, particularly with the spotted fur going across their chests.

They appeared to be arguing, complete with hisses and shrieks, about whose turn it was to do…something. Probably something so disgusting that Christine wasn't interested in learning more.

Then, another demon appeared, coming around the corner of the pile. He carried a fawn up above his head, prancing around like he was carrying a joyous gift.

Only then did Christine realize that the fawn still weakly moved.

The body was still alive.

Without waiting to consult with Ty, Christine charged.

"Keep at least one alive!" Ty had roared as Christine neatly decapitated the second demon.

Christine growled her discontent, though she knew Ty was right. They needed to capture one of these damned demons and trick it into revealing their plans.

In the meanwhile, Christine's air elemental had rescued the fawn as the demon had heaved her onto the pyre, carrying her away to the roof on the far side of one of the huts that faced the square, keeping her safe there while at the same time, not letting her see the awfulness taking place.

Were there more fawns still alive? Christine wanted to get through this group of demons so she could possibly go and rescue any living fawns. She hated to think what the poor fawns had been going through while in the clutches of the demons.

In the meanwhile, Christine turned to face the remaining two demons. She easily swung her ax first in one hand, then in the other. The two demons circled her warily, having seen the damage she'd already inflicted. Ty was facing his own demon who'd been called in to help.

How many more were there? Christine needed to finish off (or knock unconscious) at least one of the demons facing her.

"You're too late," the female demon croaked. "All the fawns are dead. Or cooked. Good eating, fawn is."

"Then why the pyre?" Christine said. "Why not roast them all?"

The demons glanced at each other as if they didn't have a good answer.

"Uh…can't eat that much meat all at once," the male

said. "Even the mighty armies don't have that many mouths."

Mighty armies. Had Lars already gathered together his armies? But that still didn't explain the pyre, and what they intended to do with it.

"You're going to lose," Christine told them. "You, and all your kind. You'll start the Great War, then you'll fail. As you always do."

The pair of demons cackled at Christine, which told her of their confidence. They circled again, keeping Christine facing the wall of burning bodies.

How many of the fawns had been alive when the fire had started?

Christine growled and rammed her ax at the female while slashing out with her hand at the male, hoping to catch it in the neck. However, he hopped back just in time.

Christine's air power growled, being kept from the fight by the injured fawn. But she couldn't split her attention. Besides, these demons were no match for her ax, if she could just catch them.

A howl suddenly erupted behind her.

Christine threw a glance over her shoulder.

Another demon had just shown up. It wasn't a minion, like the one Ty had already dispatched. No, this looked like a more important demon, complete with a huge belly, deadly tusks, red leather skin. It stood at least a head taller than Christine.

Oh shit. It also breathed fire.

And it seemed to have gotten the drop on Ty.

Christine suddenly realized that demons she'd been

fighting had purposefully kept her facing away from her friend so that the huge fiend could show up and surprise her and Ty.

She couldn't use her air power to lift the two of them up and slam them together as much as she wanted. There wasn't a handy water source close enough that she could drown them. She could throw stones at them, but it didn't seem worth the effort—she'd decapitate them soon enough.

Her fire power, however, was happy to play with the fire provided, causing long whips of living flame to suddenly lash out at the two demons.

The cackles of the demons turned to outrage that an element that *they* controlled was suddenly fighting against them. They turned away from Christine, who sprinted over to where Ty was very outclassed.

Mind you, the demon hunter knew how to fight demons, and he used that long sword to his advantage. She wished she had a moment to admire his form.

However, he had no chance with a creature who was three times his height and who blew great gouts of fire at him.

The smell of burning fur overtook the obnoxious scent of burning flesh as Christine drew closer. Then she swung into action, dropping down and chopping at the nearest leg of the demon, hoping to hit the Achilles tendon, if she was lucky.

Her luck was never that good.

This new demon had been anticipating her as he didn't merely lift his leg out of the way but then kicked out with it, nearly smacking her in the head.

Christine pivoted immediately and swung again, aiming for the back of the knee.

The demon was no longer in the same spot.

Damn, something that big shouldn't be able to move that fast!

That appeared to be the demon's specialty. One moment, he was breathing fire down her neck, then the next, he was laughing at her from halfway across the square. He also moved in a disturbing fashion, like a speeded-up film. It was so wrong it sent shivers down Christine's spine.

She could take him given time.

Time was one thing she didn't have.

The next attack wasn't directed at her, but at Ty, who couldn't move out of the way fast enough. A large claw slashed down the front of the demon hunter, through his chainmail vest, leaving a bloody trail behind.

Ty stumbled back and fell.

"No!" Christine shouted. Her earth power *slammed* into the ground, causing the demon to wobble. The demon tottered to one side as her fire power slapped him hard with living flame.

While the demon was momentarily distracted, Christine's air and water powers carried Ty out of reach, at least for the moment.

"Enough fun and games," Christine said. She bounced up, calling on her air power, so that she was close to the same height as the damned demon before she struck out with her ax.

He deflected, of course.

How could he move so fast? How could she counter it?

She called up more rocks, digging up the cobblestones of the road they stood on. As a troll, it was her natural ability to be able to hit anything she threw at, as long as there wasn't some sort of stupid shield up.

This time though, she purposefully missed with the shower of stones as it rose up. The demon skipped and leaped and hopped in that disturbing fashion it had.

And it laughed, a blood-curdling sound that might have made Christine hesitate if she hadn't been so pissed off.

How cute. The demon thought that he had *naturally* avoided all those rocks.

Christine swung her ax from hand to hand, as if she was desperately attacking, keeping all the demon's attention on her and not noticing the pile of stones that had massed like an angry hive of really wicked bees.

After another swing of her ax, Christine released the rocks from where they were poised.

No demon could avoid such a large barrage. Particularly when he thought that she'd just thrown the rocks away, not realizing that she'd been gathering them together just past where he stood.

The demon stumbled, its head bowed.

For once, Christine's luck was good enough that she was able to hit a vital artery in his neck with her ax.

The demon groaned as he fell to the earth. A muffled *whump* followed, as if most of the demon magic in the area had also just vanished.

Christine didn't have time to gloat, however. Instead, she turned and ran over to where Ty lay. The poor fawn had been squatting down next to him, but it scurried away as she approached.

Ty was still breathing, but just barely.

The claw, of course, had been poisoned.

Christine needed to get Ty to help. Now.

The only person Christine could think of was Tina. So she ported them into Tina's living room, despite how she knew that her doppelganger would bitch about the blood on her new carpet.

CHAPTER NINETEEN

Tina sat in her magical practice room, well, *not* practicing, when the call came.

The best she could describe it was a disturbance in the force.

One minute she was sitting there feeling sorry for herself, and the next minute she was on her feet, wand in hand, ready to fight whatever was coming for her.

Nothing was in the beautiful green room except herself. No demons loomed, snarling in the corner.

No trolls, either.

Speaking of trolls…

With a quick look, Tina figured out exactly where Christine stood.

And with whom.

Tina immediately closed her practice room and emerged where they were.

Ty lay bleeding to death on her new carpet, the one she'd just had to replace because she'd gotten a little careless and allowed the fire in the fireplace to leap a little too high. (Okay, so maybe she was the one who'd been a little high at the time. She'd certainly learned her lesson and was never trying pot again. Not if it caused her to lose control like that.)

"What happened?" Tina asked as she dropped to her knees. The smell of vile smoke rose up from him. "Ugh. What have you two been fighting?"

Christine stood with her ax at her feet, resting her hands against the top of the haft. "Fawns. The whole world. Dead. Demons."

Tina couldn't help but shiver. "Why would the demons attack the fawns?" she asked, incredulous. "Why didn't the fawns just drive them away?" While the fawns looked small and helpless, they could throw a wicked magical punch.

"Don't know," Christine said. She gave a choked laugh. "Maybe because they tasted good."

Tina's stomach rolled in rebellion at the realization that *that* was the smoky scent that rose up from Ty.

"Didn't know who to take him to," Christine said after a moment. "Wound's full of poison. Need to save him."

Tina nodded, realizing that Christine thought that maybe Tina could save him.

Well, she was certainly going to try.

"Just a sec," Tina said. She reached into a pocket world beside her and grabbed her wand. Then she readied herself.

She could do this. It was a simple drawing spell.

She *had* to be able to do this.

Holding the idea of what she wanted to do firmly in

her mind, Tina started the spell to draw the poison up, out of Ty's body.

For a short while, it seemed to be working. A sticky vein of sickly yellowish gunk rose up, following her hand as she slowly drew it up Ty's chest. It felt like wet spaghetti as she wrapped her fingers more tightly around it. Cold and slimy and slippery.

Tina couldn't help but smile as she realized she was actually doing it. She was going to be able to draw the poison out of Ty! She could be of help.

The next moment, the poison slipped out of her hand and slapped back down on Ty's chest, opening up a second, long wound.

"Damn it!" Christine said. "If you can't do this, tell me now. Tell me who to take Ty to."

Tina swallowed hard at the gruffness in Christine's voice. It was just because Christine was worried about Ty, not because she was angry at Tina.

"Let me try again," Tina said. She took hold of the new line of poison and started lifting it off Ty's chest. Again, the poison felt so slippery. It stretched as she lifted it. She was afraid that it would snap off and burrow deeper into Ty's flesh.

Just before the line broke, Tina gently released it so it wouldn't slap back down on Ty's skin and do more damage.

"If I had more time I could do it," Tina told Christine, though Tina wasn't certain. "I'm just not a healer."

"Then send us to one," Christine said, the impatience in her tone making Tina wince.

"Fine," Tina said. She put her wand down on the

floor, then stood and quickly sketched the outline of a door with her hands. Magic sprang up, filling the space with glistening gray mist. "Alberta will take care of you," Tina said as she stepped back and looked over to where Ty lay.

Christine had picked up Ty's body and carried it as if it weighed nothing. "Thank you," she said. Just before she stepped through the portal, she added, "Sorry for the mess."

"Don't worry about it. I'll clean it up," Tina said. "Go."

Christine gave her a single, sharp nod, then stepped through the portal.

At least Christine had still trusted Tina to create a portal for her. Though given how Tina's magic was draining away, she wasn't sure for how long she'd be able to do even that.

After Christine had left, Tina picked her wand back up again. She needed to clean the carpet now, as well as clear the air of the stench of burning flesh.

However, she merely stood there, frozen, too scared to try.

She could do this. She could clean this up. She could perform this magic.

She waved her wand.

The blood sluggishly lifted from the carpet, as if actively resisting her. It felt as though her arm was fighting to move, as if she'd been rolled in cotton batting and could no longer touch anything.

She could do this. Even if it took her the entire rest of

the day and she eventually had to resort to an actual pail and soap and water.

CHAPTER TWENTY

Lars maintained his cool when Sigmund, one of his demon generals, reported the demise of Zemund on the fawn world.

They were meeting in his newly furnished office on the human plane. The desk was a nice piece of industrial metal, made to look imposing. Lars' chair was also deliberately taller than the visitor chairs so that he'd be staring down his nose at any who came to see him.

It wasn't a throne. Not quite. But Lars could see a throne in his future, how he'd be promoted to be one of the princes of Hell when he managed to pull this off.

He hadn't started decorating the walls with heads yet. He had put up some of the maps, showing the various worlds in an artful pattern. They weren't really that close to one another, as most pocket worlds existed in their own plane and were only accessible through portals.

Lars had color-coded the maps. Red meant the attack plan was already in the can, as it were. Yellow worlds indicated those that the corruption plan had just begun.

Then there were the green worlds. Not green like grass or new leaves. No, a brown-green.

Troll green.

Lars hadn't gotten around to stashing the armies he'd accumulated on those worlds yet.

Seemed as though the time had just arrived.

"Tell me again what your minions reported to you," Lars ordered Sigmund.

"I don't know where they came from," Sigmund said gruffly. "It wasn't on my watch." Sigmund and Zemund had been brothers and shared many of the same physical attributes, such as the bright red skin, fire breathing abilities, and their speed. Sigmund, however, had been the smarter of the pair of them.

Lars didn't know if it was a good thing or a bad thing that the more intelligent of the two brothers had survived. This meeting would determine Sigmund's fate—if Lars would give him another cushy assignment like the fawns or send him against fighters likely to take a lot of lives, like trolls or orcs.

Lars made a rolling motion with his hand, indicating for the demon to just get on with his story.

"According to the minions preparing the fire, two mighty warriors came at them." Sigmund sighed. "Or at least, I think it was two. The first reports were that it had been over a dozen."

Lars nodded. That was the nature of all demons, to exaggerate their foes. Particularly when one of them had been beaten.

"One was a were-something, some sort of lap dog," Sigmund said. "Black, with a huge sword."

That would be Ty, the demon hunter, if Lars guessed right. Ty, who had been on Lars' tail. Had that been what had drawn Ty to the fawn world in the first place?

Lars had bounced through two dozen worlds after his escape from prison in order to throw off whoever would be hunting him. Some of the worlds Lars had been familiar with himself. Others, though, had been completely unknown. He'd met with demons at specific points, as arranged by his family, who could either create the next portal for him or direct him to the next demon in the chain.

It seemed that Ty had figured out that the demon meeting Lars at one of those awful rock worlds had gone straight to the fight with the fawns.

"And the other attacker?" Lars prompted Sigmund.

"A troll." Sigmund scowled, looking even more pissed off than he had been. "A troll who had magic."

Lars gave a satisfied smile. "Good. The troll is now in play."

Of course, he would have preferred that she not come onto the gameboard until later, after he'd had more opportunity to prepare.

He'd planned for her showing up, though. Had planned for those distractions specifically.

"She must have surprised my brother, or something," Sigmund said. "She couldn't have taken him in a fair fight."

"That's probably true," Lars admitted. "That damned troll can be sneaky. Now, whether or not she would have defeated Zemund anyways, well, we'll never know."

Sigmund growled but didn't say anything.

"And what about the fire? And the eruption spell?" Lars asked.

Sigmund shook his head. "They timed their attack perfectly," he said with disgust. "Zemund had just gone back to do the final rituals. If we want to use the fawn world for the spell, we're going to have to start from scratch."

Lars shook his head. "No, I need someone *reliable* to finish off the work."

"I am reliable!" Sigmund said.

"Your brother was taken out by a troll," Lars pointed out. He wasn't about to admit that the same troll had nearly killed him on more than one occasion.

"She wouldn't survive an encounter with *me*," Sigmund boasted.

Lars narrowed his eyes and stared hard at Sigmund.

The demon didn't back down. "She used rocks to pummel Zemund. And she used the bonfire itself to attack the other demons. I know that she also has magical air and water elementals. She wouldn't surprise me, not like she did Zemund."

Lars was impressed with the other demon despite himself. "All right, then," Lars said after a bit, having made his decision. "You go to the Iris world. Await orders there."

Sigmund tilted his head to one side. "But there's no fighting there," he complained.

"Exactly," Lars said. "You are distraction only. Do not engage with anyone who comes across you. Kill them if you must, but stay hidden and out of sight for the most part."

"Why would you send me there, and not to someplace where there will be proper fighting?" Sigmund asked.

Lars really was impressed with the demon's smarts. He was going to have to be careful, or Sigmund was going to be coming for Lars one of these days.

"Two reasons," Lars said. "First, when the signal comes, you will be transported to one of the other worlds where there will be more glorious battle," he assured Sigmund.

The demon nodded and waited for Lars to continue.

Patience in a demon? Interesting. Sigmund was already a general. Maybe he was bucking for the next higher position, grand general. Or even supreme general.

"Second," Lars said. "That troll you were just complaining about? May come sneaking around your encampment. I give you permission to kill her if you see her."

Sigmund gave a wicked smile. "Consider it done."

After Sigmund left, Lars first selected another easy world, like the fawns, where the demons could wreak the most havoc, then use all those souls to power the movement of his troops. It was an enhanced eruption spell: instead of lava or geysers of water, demons would erupt out of the earth.

Then he called up the other generals and had them start to deploy their troops.

The next phase of the battle had begun.

CHAPTER TWENTY-ONE

KING GARETHEN DIDN'T BRING THE HEAD OF THE cambion demons to his usual office where he met with the guard and members of the court.

Instead, the king used a tiny room, just off the kitchen, that was too small to be a proper pantry or root cellar. The cook had been paid off well, originally by the chamberlain, now by the king himself, not to blab about certain private meetings.

The room itself had good rock walls. Fresh sawdust had been sprinkled on the floor. It held three solid chairs made out of wrought iron—garden chairs, given the fancy vines and blossoms that made up the backs of the chairs. Smells from the kitchen, of the fish that had been served for lunch and the fresh corn-and-mint salad that the cook was making for dinner that night, permeated the small space.

Manny, the cambion, was just as ugly as the rest of his race. His nose constantly ran with a thick, yellow snot. His eyes were set too far apart, giving him the look of an ox.

And about as smart as one, too. Most of his skull was bald, but a few patches grew long, greasy locks of hair. Thick folds of dirty flesh encircled his neck, along with a goiter that had pushed out of one side. His eyes held the darkness of a bad nightmare, and his jagged, pointed teeth also followed that theme. He wore a dirty red vest that could barely be tied over his extended belly. Filthy claws tipped the ends of his six-fingered hands, though he only had four, equally dirty, toes.

The king wasn't sure that it had been that smart of a decision to meet with Manny alone. However, Ozlandia and Alberthendi had refused to listen to the king's very reasonable objections about how many border troops they actually needed.

Maybe they hadn't really represented the cambion's request fairly either.

"So you see," Manny continued, wheezing as he spoke, "it's really just about equal access for all."

The king shook his head. "But you have access to the other worlds through portals. Why do you need direct access to the human world through the bridge?"

Manny nodded as if he'd already considered that. "Now, you know that my people are part demon. Some of them are quite proud of their heritage. Others, they would prefer to emphasize their human halves."

"Okay," King Garethen said after a moment. He hadn't known that, though it made sense to him. While all trolls shared some traits, individuals were, after all, individual.

"The demons…" Manny paused and looked around, then over his shoulder as if making sure they were still alone. "The more purebred demons, they look down their noses at us. And the ones who would rather honor their human heritage get the worst treatment of all."

King Garethen nodded. He'd seen the same thing happen to a human-troll hybrid. Not that he'd met many. Most trolls wanted nothing to do with the humans.

"Now, you've heard about the fawns and what happened to their world, right?" Manny continued.

Grimness took over the king. He felt his heart harden. "I did." Christine had sent a messenger with the news. They'd be meeting the next day to discuss troop deployment.

Seemed that the king wasn't going to saving any coin after all on the border patrols.

Manny nodded as if in sympathy. "Shame. Real shame. I was told it was such a pretty world. Kind of like here."

King Garethen raised his eyebrows in disbelief. Most demons couldn't see the beauty in good soil and earth.

Maybe this cambion was different.

"Wouldn't want something like that to happen here," Manny said. He gave King Garethen a wink.

"Are you threatening me?" King Garethen said, sitting up taller. Of course, only a demon was stupid enough to come into the heart of Trollville and threaten the king.

"No, no, nothing like that," Manny said. "More like a trade. A deal."

"I'm listening," the king said coldly. He would listen. He'd promised that. Then he'd escort this demon right back out the door and send him on his way.

"The cambion who are more human, well, they're

going to be hurt in the oncoming war. They might even be persecuted by those who they call relatives." Manny shrugged. "It's the nature of demons to turn on their own."

King Garethen nodded slowly. While it happened sometimes among trolls, humans were the mostly likely to declare war against themselves.

"We want access to the human world, via the fairy bridge, so that those cambion who need to escape can do so quickly when the need arises," Manny said. "And in return, I can promise you that the demons will delay their attack on Trollville."

"How can you do that?" the king asked. "Even if you could make a bargain with the attacking demons, there's nothing to make them hold to their worlds."

"They'll keep their side of a bargain if enough gold has exchanged hands," Manny assured him. "And I have plenty of gold."

"Do you, now?" the king asked. Not that he needed more gold for his war chest. It was plenty full. And he anticipated a lot more coming in. As Lapundar had said— the merchants would stop complaining about taxes and would happily contribute if battles actually loomed.

"It wouldn't take much to have some of it flow here, into your worthy hands, in exchange for access," Manny said smoothly.

"Hmmm, you've given me much to think about," King Garethen replied. He wouldn't say anything more than that, and got Manny out of the palace quickly.

Then the king went back to his office, thinking.

He knew better than to make a deal with a demon,

any demon, whether they were part human or not, whether it would benefit those who were also being persecuted by the demons.

But in his private heart of hearts, King Garethen knew that he was tempted.

CHAPTER TWENTY-TWO

"Don't tell me you have to cancel," Dennis said sourly after he'd seen it was Christine calling him on his phone. "I'm already at the restaurant. Is it really too much to ask that you actually show up? Spend some time with your family?"

Dennis knew that he sounded like a sullen Jewish mother, the kind he saw in sitcoms. But the day hadn't gone anything like how he'd expected, between the fight with his boss, then the fight with traffic, followed by the near impossible task of finding parking on Capitol Hill after six PM.

Now, he was going to be here all alone at this weird Russian restaurant. The woman running it had that doughy peasant look, with blonde hair, blue eyes, and flat cheeks. To say she'd been dismissive of him was an understatement. She'd grudgingly sat him at the single separate table tucked into the far corner of the place.

The rest of the tiny space was filled with a bar along one side and three long communal tables jutting out from it. Huge guys from the rugby team of a nearby college were sitting around the one table and toasting each other with large steins of beer. Dennis didn't even know what language they were speaking in. Any one of those guys easily made up two of him. Not in height, but sheer breadth of shoulders.

What looked like a clutch of office workers crowded in around a second long table, sipping a martini-like drink that had blue food coloring in it.

Glowing blue food coloring. Which meant it wasn't food coloring but something Dennis really didn't want to know about.

He shouldn't have let Christine pick the restaurant.

"No, I am *not* canceling," Christine said with a too-familiar growl. "I'm calling to let you know I'm running a bit late but will be there as soon as I can be. Maybe ten, fifteen minutes."

"Don't tell me you're having problems parking. Oh, wait, you don't drive," Dennis said. He pressed his lips together and shook his head. He shouldn't be taking out his bad day on his sister.

"Ty was hurt," Christine said. "I'm still at the healer's."

Dennis gulped and felt even more guilty. "Get here when you can."

Damn it! Dennis stared down at his phone. If he was only going to play second fiddle, a supporting role, then he needed to change his attitude and actually be supportive.

He needed to stop feeling sorry for himself. Right the fuck now.

Dennis swallowed down the bile he'd been tasting and

looked around the room with different eyes. The walls were done in a rough-hewn wood, and the floor was concrete. It felt…rustic. Not something that Dennis was necessarily comfortable with, but he could work with this.

No TV graced any of the corners. He only now noticed that there wasn't any music in the background either. The woman who'd seated him, who still looked daggers at him from the corner next to the bar, had pointed out the menu to him, written on a chalkboard hanging over the bar.

Dennis would bet that beyond the bar was a tiny kitchen where a wizened old man performed magic. Christine might take him to some weird places, but the food was always excellent.

Slowly, Dennis rose from his seat. He telegraphed every move, trying to show that he was friendly and not threatening. He made his way over to the group of rugby players. When he had the attention of one of them, asked, "You guys mind if I join you? My sister's late."

The talk at the table died down slowly. Dennis gulped when he found that they were all staring directly at him.

He knew that stare. He'd been on the receiving end of it before. It came from the *kith and kin* who would be as happy eating a human as talking to one.

"I'll buy the next round!" Dennis said cheerily as he sat down in the space reluctantly created for him. "Oh, and my sister is the princess troll." He'd found that saying her name usually got him blank stares, but they all knew what she was. Most all of them also knew that she'd been raised a changeling.

That he acknowledged her as his sister went a long way toward easing any hostilities.

"Well, why didn't you say so at first!" said the guy on his right. "I'm Albrecto. Glad to meet you, human brother."

"Cheers!" they all said, raising their newly filled glasses.

Huh. Dennis didn't notice the waitress coming around and filling all the mugs. Or reaching over his shoulder to place the mug that was suddenly in front of him.

"Cheers!" Dennis said in return.

The beer was absolutely delicious. Cool, refreshing, with just the right amount of tang at the end.

Christine did take him to the best places.

DENNIS COULD TELL THAT CHRISTINE WAS completely baffled by the fact that he was sitting with the other patrons when she arrived. Normally, he would have continued his snit and sat by himself the whole time, getting more angry by the minute.

That was the old Dennis, he'd decided. Not the new one.

"Hey, sis!" Dennis said, waving a hand in her direction. "Come join us!"

Christine blinked, then blinked again. "Okay, who are you and what have you done with my brother?" she asked, smiling.

"I've turned over a new leaf," Dennis assured her. "Gone is the sourpuss." He knew that there would still be some rough times ahead, bad nights when he'd still feel sorry for himself. But he didn't have to live the rest of his life that way.

"Good!" Christine said.

She actually reached out and squeezed his shoulder. Christine had never been a hugger—part of her heritage of being a troll. Voluntarily reaching out and touching him was a huge show of affection from her.

The guys at the table had all grown quiet watching the exchange.

"Princess," Albrecto said. "Will you join us?"

Christine looked around the table, catching the eye of everyone seated there, drawing their attention through sheer force of will.

Dennis had seen Christine do this trick before. He remembered the shy girl who would never make eye contact. Then she put on the princess role, and suddenly she was difficult to look away from.

Badass warrior princess indeed.

"You've heard what happened to the fawns on their world," Christine said.

A shudder seemed to run around the table, touching every being there.

Dennis hadn't heard. Maybe that was what tonight's dinner was supposed to be about.

"The demons are trying to start the Great War. They've already taken many steps toward that goal. They'll succeed, unless we stop them," Christine continued. "Now, if you want to go about your celebrations, you have my blessing. If you don't want to talk about the coming war, my brother and I will go eat at a different table."

Dennis felt the shift in the mood. The guys had been celebrating a recent victory for their team. They played something like rugby but with a ball that got thrown through a stone ring set at either end of the playing field.

Oh, and how in the olden days the losers of the big tournaments would be sacrificed, their hearts eaten by the winning team to make them stronger.

Good times.

The guys looked at each other, coming to a consensus quickly.

"We would talk with you. Find out how to protect our own worlds from the attacks," Albrecto said solemnly. "Please, join us."

"Thank you," Christine said, sitting down next to Dennis. "Let us talk of war."

LATER THAT EVENING, AFTER SAYING GOODNIGHT TO their newfound friends, Christine walked with Dennis back to his car.

"That was the most amazing lamb stew I've ever had," Dennis assured Christine. It had been both hearty and sweet, spiced with peppers, sweet onions, and tangy turnips. The dessert had also been phenomenal, a cream custard with candied ginger and peppery walnuts.

"I'm glad," Christine said. She paused, then added, "Also, I need to thank you."

"For what?" Dennis asked. He looked over his shoulder at her. The badass warrior princess was gone and it was just Christine again.

"For talking with the guys back there, making friends with them before I came in," Christine said. "As a race, they aren't always the friendliest. By sitting and bullshitting with them, you gave me the opening I desperately needed in order to recruit them."

"You're welcome," Dennis said. "I didn't do it on purpose, though."

Christine cocked her head to the side. "Yes, you did. You could have sat there pissed at me the entire time."

Dennis didn't blush. That wasn't his style. Still, he acknowledged the truth of what Christine was saying. "True. But I don't need to be like that." He gave a great sigh. "I was just…I don't know. Pissed off at being second fiddle."

"What are you talking about?" Christine asked. She sounded honestly perplexed.

"I don't have some great Destiny, like you or Tina," Dennis said. "I don't have magic like Dad. I'm just… normal. Mundane. Human."

Christine drew closer to Dennis so he could see the fire in her eyes, even in the dimly lit street.

"You're my brother," Christine said. "And sometimes, yeah, you're an ass."

"Thanks," Dennis said dryly.

"But you've accepted me, and the weirdness that I bring to our family. You don't see how powerful that is. You have the strength to accept me as I am. You aren't trying to change me into something else." Christine paused. "I know it's weird, and it's hard, but by being that accepting, you make the world a better place. That isn't a second-fiddle position. Your strength—the effect you have

—is subtle, true. But its reach goes through all the planes of existence."

Dennis shook his head. It didn't feel that way.

"Plus, I do have a job for you in the coming war. Much more than what you might call a second-fiddle position."

"Really?" Dennis asked. Now it was his turn to be confused. He hadn't been able to add much to the conversation that night. The warriors had talked tactics, where to put armies, how best to fight the demons.

"What you did in there was tame a group of rowdy beastly boys," Christine said. "Brought them over to our side. The traditional allies of the *kith and kin* races are the demons, you know. Not the humans or the Host."

Dennis shrugged. "It wasn't much. I asked them questions about their rugby-like sport and tried to relate."

Christine rolled her eyes at him. "I could *not* have done that. I never played sports. A lot of the *kith and kin* are all about their games. And I'm sure you talked drinking with them. Or maybe music."

"A little," Dennis admitted, though he'd not taken them up on their offer to go and listen to some weird-ass metal band with bagpipes later that night.

"I don't know any of those subjects, how to talk about those," Christine told him. She sounded really earnest. "I can't relate to beings like you can."

"So…what are you proposing? That you want to keep taking me out to dinner?" Dennis said with a grin. "Letting me charm the natives?"

"Exactly," Christine said. "Though it's going to be a bunch of dinners. And lunches. And maybe coffee dates.

I'd say breakfasts or brunches, but most of the *kith and kin* aren't morning beings." She grimaced. "I need to build up armies quickly. Any chance I could get you to take a couple weeks off from your work? To go and be social fulltime?"

Dennis blinked, surprised. That Christine wanted to spend that much time with him was sort of astonishing. He'd had the feeling that she'd just put up with her human family since she'd been transforming herself into the badass warrior princess.

"I need you," Christine said softly. "The war effort needs you. All the worlds. Will you help?"

Dennis knew that Christine was just asking. She wasn't putting any sort of magical whammy on him to get him to go along with her.

Not that she did that sort of thing. No, only the demons did that.

"I'd be delighted to help," Dennis said. "I was born ready for this job."

Christine snorted at him. "Of course you were," she said dryly.

Dennis shrugged. In truth, he had been preparing for it his entire life. He'd learned early on how to charm a reluctant client.

Maybe that was his superpower. Not to fight the great battles, or to direct huge armies. Or even to cast magic.

But to win hearts and minds for those who did.

CHAPTER TWENTY-THREE

Vern shook his head and pushed himself back in the tall winged-back chair he always sat in when he visited Malcom's study. His limbs felt heavy, as if he'd been fighting for the last few hours. He straightened up further in his chair, feeling his muscles complaining.

"What have you been doing to me?" Vern said. He shook his head. "Sorry. Didn't mean to sound so snappish. Just. Ow."

Malcom smiled at him. "Have you started remembering your sessions yet?"

Vern automatically started to say, "No…" when it all came rushing back to him.

Malcom with the glowing eyes. They hypnotized Vern. He'd stood up, like a puppet, Malcom pulling the strings. Malcom putting a wand in Vern's hand.

Vern performing magic. Much greater magic than he'd realized was possible. He felt his magical muscles stretch and strengthen as he and Malcom worked together. That was him actually lifting great boulders up in a pocket world. Him shooting out amazingly powerful lightning bolts. Him calling up great gouts of fire.

"What have you done to me?" Vern asked again. There was something off here.

Yes, he'd had magical power. He could feel that now, could touch that sense of energy burbling through his veins.

Before this week, he would have said it was like flat fizzy water. Just a touch of effervescence remaining in it.

Now, all that energy sparkled inside him. He was afraid that if he cut himself, each drop of blood that oozed out would bubble and fizz all on its own.

Malcom gave Vern a tired smile. "War is coming," he said softly. "I wanted you to be prepared to help your daughter."

"I didn't have this much magic at the start," Vern said. He didn't know how he knew that but he was certain of it. His powers had been augmented greatly.

"True," Malcom said. He sighed and sat back in his chair. "You remember me telling you about how I started using magic?"

Vern nodded. "You said it started as a young boy."

"And that I didn't have very much magic of my own," Malcom said.

"But you do," Vern said. He could suddenly *see* how brightly Malcom glowed. He had his own inner light that was as peaceful as the man himself.

Vern's inner light was different. It was just as bright, but it was a lot harder and sharper. As though he wore a suit of great spikey armor.

Malcom shrugged. "I do have a lot of magic, but I

don't at the same time. I can't channel my own magic, not like that. Not like you and the others can. What happens is that I end up giving a lot of my power to others."

"Why would you do that?" Vern asked, offended on Malcom's behalf. "Why don't you keep it for yourself?"

Malcom laughed. "Oh, I do. I have enough for me to get by. More than that, really. But why would I hog all that power? When I can make the world better by sharing it with others?"

Vern shook his head. He still didn't understand.

"Look, I was raised poor. I know you don't see it now, but we didn't even have a pot to piss in. Had to go use the neighbor's." Malcom gave a soft laugh.

Vern didn't get the joke.

"I was raised that when you get something extra, you share it. It isn't yours. You can't just raise yourself up. You got to raise up everyone around you, bring them up with you," Malcom explained.

"Okay," Vern said. He'd certainly heard about people who had ties that strongly to their community. Vern suddenly felt ashamed that he didn't.

"You're ready now," Malcom said. "You can make a difference to the war effort. You'll also be the last person I teach. I'm too old for this, anymore."

"Thank you," Vern said. "I…I don't know what else to say. Thank you." He felt bad that he'd taken any of Malcom's power, freely given or not.

"You'll get over it," Malcom assured Vern. "Now, go win us a war."

Vern stood up. He'd never been in the army. He'd

actually been a liberal who'd made fun of the army boys, who followed orders and never thought for themselves.

However, Vern couldn't help his actions. He saluted Malcom, putting in as much heart as he could. This man deserved a medal. That he'd been preparing them all, working quietly behind the lines for all these years, humbling himself so that others could do great work, was astonishing.

Malcom slowly stood up. He looked much older than he had before, lines etched into his face, the gray seeming to have spread back from his temples.

"Thank you," Malcom said. "Whatever power I've imparted to you is in good hands. Keep it that way."

After Vern left, he still felt that bubbling of power simmering in his soul. He touched the bracelet that Christine had made for him, that protected him from demon influences.

He suddenly knew how to make it much stronger. How to protect his home better. How to take the burden off Christine for keeping her family safe.

He sent another silent thank you to Malcom.

Then he marched off to prepare for war.

CHAPTER TWENTY-FOUR

Nik silently went to fetch the potion for the Risilodans that would magically sharpen their daggers and keep the blades clean. A group of about ten of them crowded around his counter, wearing matching rugby outfits. Christine called them the rowdy boys.

He'd never seen them in here before. Normally, he primarily served human magicians. That more demons, as well as more of the *kith and kin*, were coming in, was just good for business.

Or so he told himself.

He had to remain neutral in the upcoming war. He would supply both side with potions and spell ingredients.

He did *not* sell weapons. He never had. That went against every fiber in his wooden body. He wasn't an arms dealer. Not really. Just tangentially.

The rowdy boys had the look of orcs, but they had pasty white faces, no upper tusks, and huge noses. They were also really tall, about halfway between a troll and a giant. They were as muscled as the orcs or trolls, possibly a bit more so. If Nik had to guess their heritage, he'd bet that they were a mix of orc and frost giant.

"So, one of your workers told us about this place," Albrecto, the leader, said. "She around?"

Nik instantly knew who he was talking about. "No, Christine isn't here." He didn't volunteer when she'd be there, as while he assumed that they were "friendlies" as it were, he didn't know for certain.

"That's okay," Albrecto said. "We'll be meeting up with her and the war council later tonight. Just thought we'd say hi if she was here."

"Ah," Nik said. He wasn't sure what else to say.

He'd heard about the loss of the fawn world. It had imploded after a few days, all the magic drained out of it. The few fawns who remained had gone into hiding, the demons hunting them through all the worlds.

Nik knew the spell the demons had wanted to cast using the power of all those burning fawn bodies. Or at least, he had the best guess of anyone. He'd sold the demons all the ingredients for the spell, after all.

What was different this time, compared to the last Great War, was how the demons were using their spells. Demons were generally straight forward when it came to casting. A corruption spell was good enough.

But someone—and Nik suspected it was Lars—had come up with new variations on the demon's traditional spells. Either Lars, or his cohorts, had figured out how to twist the spells. Corrupt them.

Make them into something new, something that had never been seen before.

However, Nik couldn't say anything, not to the rowdy boys, not to Christine, not to the demons he still served.

First of all, Nik *never* said anything on pure conjecture. He only spoke when he had the facts in hand. That, too, was a lesson he'd learned when he still had a human body.

And second, warning these boys of the dangers they were about to face would be violating his precious neutrality.

He did try to sell them some additional demon protection charms. That was just good business.

But he couldn't add to their conversations about what they'd be facing. The battles that awaited.

No matter how much he might want to.

CHAPTER TWENTY-FIVE

"Say that to me again. Slowly," Christine directed Ozlandia. They were standing in Christine's practice room, about to start sparring. Christine was dressed in her usual sweats and full troll form. Ozlandia wore more padding under her sweats and had her own ax at the ready. They both wore charms that provided magical shields to deflect the sharp edges of the weapons. While they could get bruised, they wouldn't cut each other to ribbons while fighting.

"We think we know which world the demons are going after next," Ozlandia said.

Christine lowered her great ax. "Where?" she demanded.

Ozlandia merely smiled at her and shook her head. "No. Not until after practice."

"Are you insane?" Christine said. "We don't have time—"

"We have time to get our troops in place," Ozlandia assured her. She pulled a sharp rock out of a pocket and tossed it at Christine, who automatically raised her ax to deflect the stone. "We practice first."

"But why?" Christine growled as she made a half-hearted attempt at a feint. Christine did *not* understand why Ozlandia was insisting on this.

Ozlandia shook her head and didn't say anything. She attacked suddenly, drawing all of Christine's attention to the fight ahead of her.

Christine found herself growling in frustration. Ozlandia had news! News that Christine could use! Why were they sparring?

When Ozlandia got through Christine's defenses yet again, striking Christine's ribs with the long wooden handle of her ax, it finally occurred to Christine that this was a different sort of practice.

Many things would go on at the same time during a battle. Some of Christine's warriors and friends were going to be fighting for their lives.

Christine *had* to be able to focus on the threat in front of her. Even when she'd rather be doing something else.

Particularly when there were other distractions.

It was difficult, but Christine narrowed her focus to the troll she battled in front of her. The tenor of their sparring changed, growing much more serious.

And more deadly.

Christine wasn't inclined to pull her punches. Not that morning. A part of her wondered if Ozlandia wanted Christine to beat the information out of her.

Slash. Pivot. Block. Strike.

For all the practice that Christine had been doing, she still wasn't as good of a physical fighter as the captain of the king's guard, who'd been practicing her entire life.

What Christine had that the others didn't was magic.

Usually, when sparring with any of the guard, Christine didn't use her magic. It was a pure physical combat. She'd practiced magical battles with Tina, until recently. Christine didn't want to think about trying to find someone else to spar magically with. Tina had to get better. Soon.

After being unable to get through Ozlandia's defenses yet again, Christine finally decided it was time to "cheat." She called up her air elemental, intending to just blow the other woman to the side.

But Ozlandia stayed standing.

Christine narrowed her eyes. It seemed that the captain of the guards had more than her usual charms to protect her that morning.

Fine.

Some part of Christine was aware that any magical being she faced would be better prepared than Ozlandia. That they'd already talked about the need for Christine to combine both her physical and magical attacks and not to think of them as separate entities.

While it had been easy for Christine to find someone to physically spar with, beings who were equipped to spar both physically and magically were hard to come by.

Christine called up her air element to throw lights at Ozlandia. Instead of the pretty strings of jewel colored lights that Christine had used before, they were a whirlwind of bright, sharp, white lights that appeared to be thrown from the center by the force of the winds.

The lights didn't have a physical component. As much as they appeared to be attacking, they weren't. They couldn't even blind an opponent, not without Christine risking being blinded herself.

They were an excellent distraction.

Ozlandia swung at the lights streaming toward her. Christine stepped through the other troll's defenses finally and whacked Ozlandia in the head with the side of her ax. Not hard enough to knock the other troll unconscious. The blow did cause the other troll to crumple onto the floor.

"Enough?" Christine asked, ax raised high, not letting her guard down. Ozlandia could be faking it, waiting for her opponent to draw close enough for another strike.

Ozlandia smiled up at Christine. "Good. You've learned."

Christine opened her mouth then shut it again. It had been one of the more difficult lessons, to not trust that a fallen enemy was actually, well, fallen.

"Enough?" Christine growled again. She would fight on if necessary. Hopefully she'd proven that she could focus when needed, and Ozlandia would actually tell her the news she had.

"Enough," Ozlandia said. She put her ax down on the floor, then pushed herself over to a wall so she could lean against it.

Christine did the same, leaning against the good solid earth. She pulled the waiting water bottles over to the pair of them as they rested, catching their breath.

"It appears that troops of demons have hidden themselves on four different worlds," Ozlandia began without preamble. "Worlds of different *kith and kin*, like the Daisilium, you know, the flower people?"

Christine gulped. Were the demons planning on attacking them? It would be as much of a slaughter as the fawns if the magic of the flower people failed. That was the primary consensus of every being she'd talked with about the fawns, that somehow the demons had overwhelmed the natural magical defenses of the fawns, making them fall back to a purely physical defense.

Hence, the complete slaughter.

"What are they doing on these worlds?" Christine asked.

Ozlandia shrugged. "They're trying to stay hidden, out of the way. They're waiting for something. Some sort of signal before they attack."

"We need to get our troops in place, then. Be ready to defend these beings," Christine said.

Ozlandia nodded. "Figured that was what you'd want to do. We'll need a lot of magical support to stay hidden like the demons, to play their waiting game."

"What would happen if we just attacked? Before they did?" Christine mused.

"The demons would then declare that *we'd* started the Great War by attacking them unprovoked," Ozlandia said, the disgust evident in her voice. "The Host might even agree with them. And that would turn some of the *kith and kin* who you've recruited against you. No, we're going to have to wait."

"All right," Christine said with a sigh. "I don't like it."

"I don't either," Ozlandia said. "I wish we had better intelligence about what the demons were actually up to.

Have you been able to figure out why they were burning the fawns? What spell would be powered by all those lives?"

"I wish I knew," Christine said. She'd asked Nik, but he wouldn't say anything, not unless he was one hundred percent certain. He'd always been like that.

Tina hadn't been much help either. She'd never been taught how to recreate demon magic or what components went into their spells, just how to fight them.

"How large are the demon armies?" Christine asked.

"Huge," Ozlandia admitted. "We're going to be thinly stretched no matter what."

Christine took a deep breath. This was it. The time of the war was coming. How could she prevent it? The demons were far too organized. It went against their very nature.

Who was the mastermind behind the new plans by the demons? Was it Lars? Had that been all he'd been doing over the five years he'd been imprisoned? Had he been the one to figure out how to oppose an opponent's magical defenses? Probably. It had that feeling.

She remembered when he'd kidnapped Tina. He'd planned on twisting—corrupting—her Destiny. He must have come up with something similar for corrupting magical defenses.

He was a greater enemy than she'd ever given him credit for.

Hopefully she'd prepared enough to beat him before the war began.

CHAPTER TWENTY-SIX

BUDDY CAVORTED ALONE IN THE THRONE ROOM, shaking his fat ass and letting his big belly hang out. The rock walls glowed with barely contained lava. Boulders in the corner steamed. Ash filled the air like confetti. The lovely sound of screams echoed throughout the room, piped in from Buddy's personal torture chamber.

It appeared that Lars might actually pull this off.

All the other beings had been shocked at the slaughter of the fawns. It was all the *kith and kin*, as well as the Host, appeared to be talking about.

They'd missed the entire death of the grassland beings. Lars had managed to pull that one off without anyone being the wiser. While their deaths wouldn't power as strong of an eruption spell, at least the spell could be completed.

Then again, the grassland beings traveled even less frequently than the fawns. And they kept their world closed to most visitors. They'd deliberately trapped themselves on their own plane.

In order to travel to their plane, you had to be invited by one of the grassland beings. The chances of someone stumbling on their deaths before the right time was even smaller than finding out that the fawns were gone.

Buddy still wasn't certain exactly how Lars had managed to get onto their plane. He must have corrupted some other spell.

No matter.

Today, Buddy could taste victory. And it smelled even sweeter than his own farts.

His PR machine was all set to send out victory dispatches. Particularly since Lars had managed to get the enemy distracted.

Buddy danced around the throne room again, his bare, clawed toes clicking against the rocks, his snout belching tiny flames and smoke.

Of course, Buddy had a second set of dispatches also prepared, in case Lars *didn't* succeed. The victory set was all about how Buddy had put Lars into the right position so that *they* could be successful.

The other set was all about how Buddy had tried to caution the young hotheaded demon about such a foolish attack, even as he'd supplied the troops.

Buddy hadn't been this excited about a battle since the old days of the first Great War.

He may, *may*, even have to join with the other demons on the battlefields.

Only if they were winning, of course.

Buddy still wasn't looking forward to having to crown another prince of hell. He also knew that Lars wouldn't be satisfied with anything less.

Not unless Buddy was able to somehow temper Lars' victory…

He'd have to put some thought into that. Buddy wouldn't be helping his enemies. It was pure self-interest.

In the meanwhile, maybe he should order tacos for everyone. Again. Because what better way to celebrate than with meat that was spicy enough to burn the tongue?

CHAPTER TWENTY-SEVEN

"I can't help," Tina said. Damn it. She didn't want to cry again. Not even in front of Christine.

They sat in the beautiful breakfast nook of the townhouse Tina shared with her two roommates. They were both at their jobs. (Ugh, was she going to have to get one of those? If she couldn't support herself magically?) The back of the building looked over a lovely green area full of pines, big-leaf maples, and oaks. Down at the bottom of a slight hill ran a small creek. The frogs sang along with Tina's grief at night.

"But why?" Christine asked, clearly puzzled. "We need you. If we don't have more magical support, we're not going to be able to hide or be ready for when the demons attack."

Tina signed. "My magic…it's draining away. Quickly. Even the simplest spell is slipping away."

"I'm so sorry," Christine said. She wore her human doppelganger look that day.

For Tina, it was like looking into a dark mirror. Their

faces had almost the same bone structure, though Christine's was a touch wider and broader. However, their noses, lips, eyes, were all the same. Just that Christine's coloring was much darker, with brown hair instead of blonde, brown eyes instead of blue, and much darker skin compared to Tina's pale white.

Their outfits were opposite as well. Christine wore an emerald colored T-shirt over light-blue jeans, while Tina wore a black shirt and black jeans.

"Have you talked with Malcom?" Christine asked after a moment.

Tina shook her head. "I can't. I can't ask or tell anyone. You're the only one who knows the extent of it."

"You've got to get help," Christine said gently. Well, as gently as a troll could. Tina knew Christine meant well.

"No one can help me," Tina said. "People don't just lose their magic this way."

Christine gave Tina a sharp look. "Then it might not be you." She paused, then added, "I hate to ask this, but is there a chance that you're being influenced by demons?"

"No," Tina snapped immediately. "Not a chance. That was one of the first things I checked. All my magical defenses are in place."

"The fawns probably thought their magical defenses were in place. But the demons still overwhelmed them. I think you should check again. Or have someone else check for you," Christine insisted.

Tina shook her head.

"See? That's what I mean," Christine said. Anger tinted her tone, making Tina feel even more isolated.

"I don't understand," Tina said after a moment.

Christine paused, as if trying to find the right words. "You are reacting as if you're depressed," she said slowly.

"Of course I'm depressed! My magic's disappearing! My magic is my only reason for living!" Tina said, starting to get angry as well.

"See? That's the Tina I know. Not this mopey teenager full of 'woe is me' and angst," Christine said. "You need to fight this, Tina. I know you can. This isn't you."

Tina took a deep breath. "It just feels like I'm pushing a dead weight up a hill," she admitted.

Christine nodded. "That's the depression. Something is influencing you. Something demonic. You need to get out of the house. Go visit Malcom. Hell, go and see your parents. When was the last time you left this place?"

Tina thought for a moment. "The last time we had dinner together," she said after a moment. That had been over a month ago.

"And you haven't left the townhouse since?" Christine asked.

"No…" Tina said.

"That's not like you either," Christine said flatly.

"But I don't want to leave!" Tina said. She heard the scared wail in her tone. "I'm afraid to leave."

Christine stood up. "You need to get help."

"But—"

"No," Christine said. "No more excuses. You need to get help. Not just sit here in the dark, moping."

"You don't understand," Tina said.

"Yes, I do. Better than anyone else," Christine replied. "Remember that changeling spell that kept me afraid of going out, afraid of leaving my apartment, afraid of trying anything new? The same thing's been cast on you. You need to fight it."

Tina heard the "or else" at the end of that statement. Tina wasn't sure what Christine's "or else" would entail. She didn't dare ask.

After Christine had left, Tina opened up the windows looking out on the green area. She took several deep breaths of the cleansing air.

She would make herself get up. To leave her townhouse. To go walk in the sunshine, or even the rain.

Maybe tomorrow.

CHAPTER TWENTY-EIGHT

Ty groaned as he tried, and failed, to push himself up. Again.

Damn, that hurt. That demon had slashed him, then poisoned him, but good.

He lay on the couch in his tiny studio apartment. While hunting demons paid well, Ty also spent a lot of money on equipment and spell ingredients. He could probably afford something bigger—his savings account was rounding out nicely—but he didn't see the point. He was rarely here, spending most of his time either hunting or in court, testifying.

At least this was a nice place to convalesce for a while. Wood parquet covered the floor, warm and polished. Sun streamed in through the southern-facing windows, as did the traffic noise from the busy street just outside. Ty lived on the ground floor. He wasn't worried as much about demons coming through the wide windows to get him as he was about being able to get out without breaking his fool neck by living on the top floor or something.

The kitchen contained a compact four-ring cooktop, an oven that was just as small, a microwave, a sink, and maybe two feet of countertop. All of it was spotless. For Ty, it was perfect, as he generally went out to eat. Or had food delivered. It was one of the advantages of living on Capitol Hill.

To the right of the couch lay Ty's bed, tucked into a corner. He'd slept on a fold-out bed for years. However, too often he'd ended up just crashing on the couch, ending up with cricks in his neck and his back being thrown out. Though this apartment was barely four hundred square feet, he'd still splurged on a real (single, extra-long) bed as well as a couch he could stretch out on.

He was getting tired of staring at the same four walls. At least Christine had come by to see him earlier.

He'd hated to disappoint her, but he couldn't join the battle. Not yet. Not until he'd recovered.

He hadn't admitted to her just how much Tina's "help" had ended up damaging him. The second line of infection was much worse than the original claw mark. Seemed that Tina's magic had accelerated the spread of the poison.

That girl was trouble. He'd always thought so, particularly after seeing how Christine had blossomed over the past few years, growing far beyond her human doppelganger.

Still. Ty managed to push himself up to seated, swinging his legs heavily to the floor.

He'd assured Christine that he'd join the battles later.

Because Ty had a bad feeling about all of this.

War was coming.

And he was on the sidelines, at least for now.

CHAPTER TWENTY-NINE

King Garethen tried to pay attention to what Manny was saying. However, his eyes kept flickering over to the trunks of gold lining the walls of the little root cellar they met in.

Trunks. Half a dozen of them. Each about three feet by two feet, and a foot tall. Filled to the brim with gold coins. Or beautiful gems and jewels.

King Garethen could smell the wealth contained in those trunks.

He'd met with Manny several times now, always listening to the cambion's pleas, how scared he was for his people now that war was imminent.

They just needed access to the human plane. And quickly, too, so that the cambions who were more human than demon would have a place to escape to when the full demons came calling.

It was a charity action, really, that the king was considering. Something that not only wouldn't harm Trollville, but would actually help it in the long run, given the amount of coin that he was getting for such a little thing.

It did mean going behind Princess Kizalynn's back. Not that she'd ever find out about it. The king would make sure of that.

He was doing the right thing here, despite the niggling worry that somehow he was being tricked.

He couldn't see where the trick was, though. The protection spells that he'd set up still held. He wasn't being influenced by the demons as far as he could tell.

No, he was just looking the other way when they came through Trollville, on their way elsewhere.

Demons—and in particular, the cambions—wouldn't dare to stay inside the borders of Trollville. He trusted the trolls to be able to take care of themselves if there were any demons stupid enough to linger.

"So do we have a deal?" Manny asked. He was still a disgusting example of a being, with his dripping snot, the hair sprouting from his various warts slimy with grease, his eyes as mesmerizing as an abyss.

Slowly, cautiously, King Garethen nodded. "We need to go over the latest changes to the contract," the king said. "But I think that the last few details can be smoothed out."

He didn't like the suddenly gleam in Manny's eye.

And he really didn't like having to lean over and shake Manny's hand.

Nothing really bad would come of this, or so the king assured himself.

Plus, all that gold…

CHAPTER THIRTY

Lars kept a serious mien, though he felt like chortling, or even cavorting.

Stupid princess troll had taken the bait. She'd sent her armies into the untethered planes, stripping many of the *kith and kin* worlds of their natural defenses and fighters.

She had no idea the Hell that Lars was about to unleash.

Lars still wore his human form, working from the office that had gradually taken shape. The maps on the walls were covered with pins, showing where his armies waited. Lines led from the pins to the other planes, where the battles would actually take place. His desk was littered with memos from the awaiting generals, all chomping at the bit, wanting to finally get on with it.

That had been one of his biggest victories, not just to get the various generals into place, but to get them to actually *agree* to his plan instead of them acting out and starting mayhem on their own.

Of course, the longer that Lars waited, the greater the chance that someone would jump the gun.

Lars couldn't afford to wait too long. He just needed for Christine to get herself into place as well. Instead of staying safely here on the human plane, or even in Trollville (though wouldn't she be surprised when she learned what her uncle had been up to?)

The corrupted corruptions spells were working beautifully. No one even suspected the demonic influence that was taking place.

True, the trolls had been a lot harder to corrupt than most. It had taken several of the seemingly innocuous gifts to be placed in the Hall of Viewing before the king had started to be influenced at all.

But he'd finally fallen under the demonic spells, as had most of the rest of the beings Lars and his minions had focused on.

All Lars had to do now was to give the order.

As soon as Christine was in place, or rather, out of place, he would do just that.

And the Great War would begin.

CHAPTER THIRTY-ONE

CHRISTINE HADN'T WANTED TO LEAVE THE HUMAN plane. It would be better for her to direct her armies from there rather than traveling to the *kith and kin* planes. In terms of communications, it was much simpler for her to be in a single location, for messengers to come to her rather than having to track her down.

However, what kind of general never visited, let alone fought, beside her own troops? That may have been acceptable for human armies, but not for Christine, and particularly not for the *kith and kin*. It was a matter of trust as much as anything else.

Christine had personally recruited many of the *kith and kin* armies. They needed to see her mettle. Staying behind the lines of fire would cause them to question their choices.

So Christine arranged a tour, visiting the various troops on the planes where they'd been stationed. Not all were on the planes where the demons were located. She'd also sent them to the worlds that were considered the most vulnerable, places where the beings relied primarily on a magical defense and weren't physical fighters.

She was on the last of those planes now—Daisilium— the world of the flower people.

It was a lovely world, though a bit too warm for Christine's tastes. She preferred the clouds and rain of Seattle. Very few forests interrupted the endless green fields. Hills gently undulated across the plains, nothing sharp or steep. Christine had never realized how too much of the same bothered her. Her eyes kept skipping around, looking for some kind of variety in the landscape.

Still, the air here smelled good, of fresh grass, good earth, and bitter pollen. Breezes kept away some of the heat caused by the burning sun. The greenery of the world brightened Christine's heart.

The flower people themselves were willowy. Their hair stood out around their heads like petals, usually white, though some were orange or even purple. Their bodies seemed to be composed of brown and green vines.

One of the things that Christine found most disturbing about the flower people was that she could never predict where a limb might be coming from. While the flower people sort of had a front and a back, any of the vines that made up their bodies could detach itself and become something like a hand or a foot.

Christine had never met any of the flower people before. They rarely traveled, and in the past five years while she'd been the guardian for the fairy-bridge, she'd never seen one.

The demons were still grouped just under the trees to the south. Christine's people had them surrounded. The flower people kept the army of the *kith and kin* hidden. They were very good at illusions. Christine doubted that the demons even knew that anyone else was there.

However, the demons weren't going to be able to escape and attack the Daisilium, not without fighting through an army of the *kith and kin*.

Christine was too aware of how outnumbered her armies were. Even here, the demons outnumbered her fighting force two to one. Many of the *kith and kin* races hadn't come to her side. They felt that while they might not owe a strong allegiance to their old allies the demons, they didn't want to actively fight against them.

Christine wondered sometimes about the old saying of how all it took for evil to flourish was for good men to do nothing.

Would the insistence of so many races of the *kith and kin* to remain neutral be their downfall?

Christine was just finishing her review of the troops. Most of the beings here were the rowdy boys, who were tall and pale, always cracking jokes. Their magic was related to cold and freezing things, which made sense, as Christine suspected that they had some frost giant blood in them.

Mainly though, the rowdy boys were fierce fighters, depending on a physical attack. Their primary weapon were huge wooden clubs, six or eight feet tall. Frequently, the wood was reinforced with a bar of metal in the middle of it, and they had a spiked head as well. They used a variant of their fighting club in one of their many sports. This one was similar to a hockey stick and involved knocking a ball around on an ice field. That they also were allowed to bash in each other's heads while playing seemed to be just a side benefit.

Ozlandia stayed at Christine's side. She wasn't there as a bodyguard—Christine could take care of herself, thank you very much. Ozlandia's presence primarily gave Christine more of an air of legitimacy. Christine herself was an important person. Of course, she'd have a guard. That Ozlandia was the head of the guard for the king of the trolls gave Christine greater stature.

Christine wasn't great at the politics or war, but she was getting better at it.

One of the demons appeared at the edge of the woods just as Christine was getting ready to go.

Wait. She knew that demon. He was tall and red, and looked almost exactly like the demon she'd fought at the world of the fawns, with a huge belly, deadly tusks, and red leather skin.

And he was staring directly at her.

"We have a problem," Christine said, interrupting the latest joke from the head of the rowdy boys.

"What do you mean?" Gilmasso asked, looking around. "The other team hasn't come to steal the ball, has it?" He looked over his shoulder at the long string of rowdy boys with a grin.

"No," Christine said. She'd already expressed her fear that the rowdy boys would be too busy with their games that they'd be caught unaware when the battle actually started.

Ozlandia said quietly over Christine's shoulder, "I see him."

While the rest of the demons went about their

business—desecrating trees, sharpening weapons, and farting—the one demon continued to stare at them.

And now he'd taken a step out from under the trees. Directly toward them.

"You ready?" Christine asked Gilmasso as she reached for the ax that was still tied to her back.

"Ready? I was born ready," Gilmasso bragged.

Christine couldn't help but roll her eyes. Of course, the rowdy boys would use that phrase.

Gilmasso's second in command blew a piercing whistle in a complicated pattern, long notes punctuated by short, sharp tweets.

A growl followed the call to action. Christine found it very satisfying. It held a predatory note that she recognized and responded to with her own loud rumble.

The demons under the trees all seemed to wake up and realize their predicament. They started pointing at the various troops, shouting obscenities both at them as well as at each other.

The demon general nodded and started striding directly toward Christine.

"Is this it?" Ozlandia asked.

Christine shook her head. "No. This is just a skirmish," she said as she readied herself.

This wasn't the start of the Great War. Just a prelude.

What happened next would possibly determine the rest, though.

CHRISTINE'S FRUSTRATION BUILT AS THE DAMNED

demon general stepped around her attack again. She knew from the start that he couldn't be taken out with a physical attack alone.

However, the stupid demon had come prepared. Her wind attacks had been ignored, canceled by some charm he wore. Same with her water attacks. (Though shooting him full in the snout every time he was about to cast a gout of fire had at least neutralized that attack of his. Plus, it had been great fun to see his puzzled look when he realized his fire couldn't get through.)

While Christine could blast the demon with fire, he was naturally immune to it as he breathed fire himself.

The best attack she'd managed had been disrupting the earth under his feet. She hadn't been able to trick him with rocks or lights, getting him to turn his focus on anything but her.

It was as though he'd studied her, learned her techniques and attacks, and had come prepared.

Christine hadn't expected that at all. Particularly not from a demon.

What could she do that was unexpected? And sneaky? And fast?

The battle raged on all sides of her, the rowdy boys laughing as they smashed in the heads of demons. However, the demons kept coming. It was as if every one that the boys took out, another two took their place.

Was it magic? Or had they just miscounted? Had there been a lot more demons hiding in the woods?

Christine knew that while the demons would fight on once their general was dead, they'd be a lot easier to take down.

Ozlandia fought her own demon, probably the second in command to the general. He was tall, blue, with great wings and a long, horned snout. He spat acid, a lovely trait that had singed Christine's armor as well.

Christine tried with another air attack, just to see if she could get the demon she faced to turn even slightly.

But her air attack wasn't as strong as she'd intended. Instead of a gale, it came out more like a light summer breeze.

Damn it! The demons *were* neutralizing the magic around them. How were they doing that? No one who Christine had talked with were even aware of how to do such a thing.

Christine took a running leap at the general, intending a kicking attack. He swatted her away, as she'd intended.

In the few moments it took for him to close with her again, she looked around.

No ice existed on the field of battle.

Which meant that the demons weren't merely blocking her magic, but all magic.

Christine dropped a string of lights where she stood. It wasn't much. The lights themselves shone feebly, as if they'd been covered by a thick fog. They wouldn't float in the air, either, but crept along the ground, heading slowly for the demon.

It was the best she could do. Since the demon seemed so focused on her, she could use that to her advantage.

Christine swung her great ax with the flat side, intending to merely bash the demon's leg.

He stepped nimbly out of the way. At least he didn't

move as fast as his brother, though he still had that disturbing fast-film look when he moved quickly.

The demon returned the favor, and kicked at Christine, forcing her to back away.

Damn, he was fast. And big. And he had a much longer reach than Christine.

What could she do? How could she win?

Could she win?

Christine growled low and deep in her chest.

She could fight. And not just the demon in front of her, but the negative thoughts suddenly floating around her.

More demon magic.

They were *not* unstoppable. They were not immortal or destined to win.

Her troops could kill them.

As could she.

Christine slashed out with her ax, swinging it from one side to the other, as if harvesting wheat with it, forcing the demon back.

He glanced down when he realized he'd stepped close to her creeping line of lights.

He laughed, he actually *laughed*, as he stomped his foot down.

Christine kept her scowl, despite how perfectly the sound effect worked, and a tinkling breaking glass noise filled the air.

The demon laughed again and stomped down on more of the lights.

Perfect.

While the demon had been distracted by the pretty

lights, he'd ignored that they were strung together by a rope.

With her air power, Christine quickly wrapped the rope around the demon's ankles. He couldn't kick out and break the binding, or even run away. He had to stay still.

When he leaned over to slash at the rope with his claws, Christine leaped into the air with her mighty ax and came down, swinging the ax sideways and slashing at the demon's exposed throat.

With a muffled *whump*, the demon crumpled and fell to the side.

Christine jumped over the legs of the demon and attacked again, from behind, not giving the demon a chance to reach her with his still-deadly claws.

She couldn't quite sever the head from the body with a single blow. His damned spinal cord was too thick for that. But she put enough of a gash across his throat that he'd never rise again.

A shock wave went across the battlefield when the general of the demons died.

Christine expected the fighting to grow more desperate as the demons fought on.

She had not expected them to retreat immediately, racing toward the trees.

Did they expect to use some sort of portal and escape?

Christine's troops raced after the demons, as did Christine and Ozlandia. They had to see where the demons were going to next.

Christine didn't bother fighting the few stragglers she passed. Sure, she swiped at them with her ax. But she let the rowdy boys who were following her take care of them.

The smell of filth and corrupted earth nearly made Christine retch. What the hell had the demons been doing?

A wide circle of trees had been cut down, the demons making an unnatural clearing. In the center of the clearing lay a vast, dark hole. It was at least twelve feet in diameter. A swirling blackness filled the center of it, sickly and foreboding.

The demons streamed by where Christine and Ozlandia had paused, leaping into the dark portal.

Where were they going? Why would they leave so suddenly?

Christine had to find out.

She shouted over to one of the rowdy boys, "Stay here! Guard against any who may return!"

He nodded and started organizing his fellows.

Then Ozlandia, with a grim nod, grabbed onto Christine's arm.

Christine twisted her hand so that she could clasp Ozlandia's arm in return. They each held their great ax in the other hand.

As one, they stepped into the abyss.

———

CHRISTINE LOOKED AROUND HER WITH SURPRISE.

The demon portal had landed them in the plane of the Kimukaki, one of the first warrior races who had joined Christine's army. The Kimukaki were a proud race, with white, dog-like faces, ears that hung down like a beagle's, and fierce claws.

Why would the demons come here? The Kimukaki were primarily physical fighters. They had minor magic.

The town was cute, with tall, skinny wooden buildings and many open windows (the Kimukaki loved hanging their heads out of windows and sniffing mightily at any and all breezes.) The street itself was paved with red brick. Dancing fountains marked every other intersection.

The fighting in the street was fierce. Kimukaki of all sizes had already joined in, from the littlest pup to the oldest grandmother.

The ground rumbled, as if a slight earthquake had just occurred.

Suddenly, a second black portal opened up just a few blocks down from where Christine and Ozlandia stood. More demons came pouring out.

Though Christine couldn't see a third portal opening, she still felt the ground tremble, announcing its presence.

Suddenly, she realized her mistake.

The demons had never been planning on attacking in the places where they'd started. Those camps had been a distraction.

Christine had fallen for it, too. She'd stripped some of the planes of the *kith and kin* of their fiercest fighters, moving them out of place, so that they wouldn't be able to protect their home worlds or their people.

Frustrated at being duped, Christine made the outline of a door with her hands, intending on creating a portal to take her back to the world where most of the Kimukaki were stationed.

Her magic fizzled.

The only way out was through one of the demon portals.

She belatedly recalled that the Kimukaki, like most of the *kith and kin* worlds, had isolated themselves, thinking that they'd be protected.

The demons had obviously found a way around that. It struck Christine that the spell they'd used for the portal was similar to the spell used to cause eruptions of lava.

Only it had been twisted for eruptions of demons.

"Do we fight?" Ozlandia asked quietly.

Christine shook her head. "We have to get out. We have to get the word out. The demons are attacking all the worlds that we drew warriors out of."

Ozlandia shuddered. She threw a questioning look at Christine, who slowly nodded.

"Yes. We've failed. The Great War has begun."

READ MORE!

Be sure to read all the books in the Seattle Trolls series!

The Changeling Troll
The Princess Troll
The Fairy-Bridge Troll
The Troll-Demon War
The Troll-Human War
The Troll-Troll War

Available for sale now!

ABOUT THE AUTHOR

Leah Cutter writes page-turning fiction in exotic locations, such as a magical New Orleans, the ancient Orient, Hungary, the Oregon coast, rural Kentucky, Seattle, Minneapolis, and many others.

She writes literary, fantasy, mystery, science fiction, and horror fiction. Her short fiction has been published in magazines like *Alfred Hitchcock's Mystery Magazine* and *Talebones*, anthologies like Fiction River, and on the web. Her long fiction has been published both by New York publishers as well as small presses.

Find Leah's books here.

Follow her blog at www.LeahCutter.com.

Reviews

It's true. Reviews help me sell more books. If you've enjoyed this story, please consider leaving a review of it on your favorite site.

Come someplace new…

Are you a traveler? Do you enjoy exploring strange new worlds, new cultures, new people?

Sign up for my newsletter and I'll start you on your travels with a free copy of my book, *The Island Sampler*.

I will never spam you or use your email for nefarious purposes. You can also unsubscribe at any time.

http://www.LeahCutter.com/newsletter/

ABOUT KNOTTED ROAD PRESS

Knotted Road Press fiction specializes in dynamic writing set in mysterious, exotic locations.

Knotted Road Press non-fiction publishes autobiographies, business books, cookbooks, and how-to books with unique voices.

Knotted Road Press creates DRM-free ebooks as well as high-quality print books for readers around the world.

With authors in a variety of genres including literary, poetry, mystery, fantasy, and science fiction, Knotted Road Press has something for everyone.

Knotted Road Press
www.KnottedRoadPress.com

www.ingramcontent.com/pod-product-compliance
Lightning Source LLC
Chambersburg PA
CBHW070639100726
47907CB00007B/2035